CHEER USA!

CHEER USA!

Fight, Bulldogs, Fight!

By Jeanne Betancourt

AN
APPLE
PAPERBACK

SCHOLASTIC INC.
New York Toronto London Auckland Sydney
Mexico City New Delhi Hong Kong

Thank you to Janine Santamauro Knight and Doreen Murphy, cheerleading coaches at St. Joseph by the Sea.

Cover illustration by Karen Hudson

ISBN 0-590-97808-X

12 11 10 9 8 7 6 5 4 3   9/9 0 1 2 3 4/0

Printed in the U.S.A.   40
First Scholastic printing, November 1998

For Carole Halpin

Emily Granger took her blue-and-white cheerleading uniform out of its plastic bag. She held up the uniform and smiled to herself. She was a Claymore Middle School cheerleader, and she was going to wear her uniform for the first time. Today was the big pep rally, and the CMS cheerleaders were wearing their uniforms all day. Emily couldn't wait to get to school.

She put on her skirt and pulled up the zipper. It stopped halfway up. Was it broken? She pulled again. It still wouldn't close. She tried to button the waistband. At least two inches separated the button from the buttonhole. But yesterday it fit, Emily thought. I must have gotten bigger overnight!

She tried on the top. It was too small.

Emily mentally listed what she'd eaten since she'd tried on her uniform at school the day before. Last night she'd had a second helping of garlic mashed potatoes with fried chicken. There was apple pie with ice cream for dessert. And a couple of cookies and some milk before bed. Today she'd already had a pancake breakfast. Tears filled her eyes. She ate too much and had gotten so fat overnight that this morning her uniform didn't fit!

The door to Emily's room flung open. Lily, her

1

four-year-old sister, came running in. Lily had on a miniature version of the CMS cheerleaders' uniform, the same one Emily had worn when she was Lily's age.

Lily twirled around. "I'm a cheerleader!" she shouted. "I'm going to the pep rally. Mom said."

The entire Granger family was involved in CMS sports. Even the Granger dog! Emily's mother and her older sister, Lynn, had both been captains of the CMS cheer squad. Her father and brother played CMS football and basketball. And starting when Emily's father was a kid, the Granger family had owned and raised the CMS bulldog mascot. Over the years there had been three Granger bulldogs. Now they had Bubba IV, great-grandson of Bubba I.

Bubba IV followed Lily into Emily's room.

Emily squatted to give Bubba a hello pat and her sister a kiss. "You look great," Emily told Lily. "It finally fits you."

"I'm a big girl," bragged Lily.

Me, too, thought Emily. Only I'm *too* big.

Lynn poked her head in the door.

"Lily, Mom wants you to go eat breakfast," she said. "Hey, Em, you got your uniform! Let me see."

Emily was embarrassed to show her perfect sister how imperfectly her uniform fit.

"Hurry," Lynn insisted. "Stand up."

As Emily stood she saw the look of surprise on her sister's face.

"It's too small," Emily told her, the tears coming back to her eyes. "It fit yesterday, but now it's too small."

Lynn smiled.

"It's not funny!" Emily told her.

"Emily, that uniform could not possibly have fit you yesterday," Lynn said. "No one grows that much overnight."

"I ate a lot for dinner last night," Emily confessed. "And I had a big breakfast, too."

"It must be someone else's uniform," Lynn told her. "All you have to do is figure out whose it is. I'm sure that girl has yours." She patted Lily on the head. "Come on, Lily."

The little cheerleader took Lynn's hand and they left the room. Bubba didn't follow them. Instead he licked Emily's leg and whimpered. Bubba always knew when Emily was feeling sad.

"Oh, Bubba," Emily said. "What if it *is* my uniform?"

Bubba lay down on the rug, dropped his head on his folded paws, and watched Emily.

Emily looked at the blue-and-white pleated cheerleader's skirt. Yesterday, Coach Cortes handed out uniforms after cheerleading practice, and the whole squad tried them on. Like the other cheerleaders, Emily had put her uniform back in the plastic bag to take home. Then she went with Melody and Joan to Squeeze, the juice bar, for something to drink. That's when we must have mixed up uniforms, thought Emily. Melody and I are about the same size. But Joan is so much smaller than I am. Emily hoped that she was holding Joan's uniform.

She grabbed the phone and speed-dialed Joan.

DELHAVEN DRIVE 7:45 A.M.

Joan Russo-Chazen practiced a tuck jump in front of her bedroom mirror. She loved how the skirt of her cheerleading uniform flew up in the air. She was doing a back standing handspring across the rug when she heard a knock on her door. It was her father telling her she had a phone call.

That was a close call, Joan thought as she ran down the stairs to the only phone in the house. If my father had opened my door he'd have seen me doing a handspring in my uniform. He'd figure out that cheerleaders do gymnastics, and my cheerleading career would end before it began.

Joan's parents were anti most sports, especially sports in which people could be injured. They wouldn't let Joan take gymnastics or her older brother, Adam, play football. Adam didn't care because he didn't want to play football. But I care, thought Joan. I care because I love cheering, especially the tumbling. The only lucky thing about my parents being antisports is that they don't know that cheerleaders do lots of gymnastics.

"Hello?" Joan said into the phone.

It was Emily. She told Joan that they had each other's uniforms.

"But I have my uniform on," Joan told her, "and it fits perfectly. Maybe you have Melody's."

After Joan hung up the phone she ran back upstairs to fix her hair. As she ran up the stairs, her mother was coming down. She held up a hand to stop Joan.

"I can't believe my eyes," she said. "This is *my* daughter in a cheerleading uniform?" She said it with disapproval, as if wearing a cheerleading uniform was some kind of crime. "It totally baffles me that you want to shout and jump around for a bunch of boys fighting over a ball."

"I love football," Joan told her. "And I love cheering."

"Indeed," said her mother. "What time will you be home?"

"The team and cheerleaders are going to Bulldog Café after the pep rally," Joan said. "Adam's invited, too. Then Emily asked me to sleep over."

"Yes to the gathering at the café," her mother

said. "No to sleeping over. Maybe another time. I'll pick you up on the way back from the university," she added. "That will be around six."

Ms. Russo continued down the stairs. "Cheerleading," she mumbled. Joan couldn't understand the rest of the sentence, because her mother was muttering to herself in German — one of the languages she taught at the university.

Joan bounded up the rest of the stairs. She was disappointed that her mother wouldn't let her stay over at Emily's, but she wasn't surprised.

She wouldn't let that ruin her first pep rally.

DOLPHIN COURT APARTMENTS 8:00 A.M.

Melody Max was about to put on her cheerleading uniform when Emily phoned and asked her if she had the right uniform.

"I haven't put it on yet," she told Emily. "Hold on, I'll try it." Melody lay the phone on her bed and slipped the top over her head. It was too big. She stepped into the skirt and zipped and buttoned it. It was at least a size too large. Melody picked up the phone and told Emily, "It's too big on me. It must be yours."

Emily's heart sank. Her uniform was too big for Melody. I must be so fat, Emily thought.

"I'll meet you at our lockers so we can exchange before school," she told Melody. "I'll leave in a few minutes."

After Melody hung up the phone she wondered why Emily didn't sound happier that the mystery of the mixed-up uniforms had been solved. Maybe she just wants to be sure it's hers, she decided.

"Hey, sugar," Melody's mother called from the kitchen. "When are you going to show me that uniform of yours? I have to go to work."

Melody went to the kitchen, showed her the uniform, and explained about the mix-up with Emily.

"My, my," chuckled her mother. "She must have had a fright when she put on yours. Sorry I wasn't here when you went to bed last night. It's taking a while to get the newspaper the way I want it. Part of being the new editor, I guess. I'll try to be home early tonight."

"But I won't be here," Melody said. "There's a party at the café after the pep rally. And then I'm sleeping over at Emily's, remember?"

"Right," said her mother. "Is the big game with the Santa Rosa team tomorrow?"

"Next week," Melody told her. "We're having the pep rally today so we can keep building school spirit all next week."

"I'll be sure to be there," her mother said.

"The rivalry with Santa Rosa is certainly a big deal in Claymore."

Melody kissed her mother good-bye and went back to her room to get her books. It was great that her mother would see her cheer at the big Bulldog-Cougar game. She just wished her father could be there, too.

She picked up a framed photo from her desk. Her mother and father had taken her skiing in Colorado last winter and asked a stranger to take their picture when they finished their first run down the mountain. Her parents, each with an arm around Melody, looked so happy in that picture. Two months later they told her they were divorcing, and a week later her father moved out. Three months after that her mother was offered a job as editor of the *Claymore News*.

Melody's father was a meteorologist and television weather announcer in Miami. Her parents agreed that Melody should leave Miami with her mother and move to Claymore on the west coast of Florida for the three years of middle school. After that she could move back to Miami to live with her father while she went to high school. But for now Melody would only be with her father for an occasional weekend and during vacations.

She missed being with both her parents. It

was hard to believe that they would never be a family like that again.

She put the frame back on her desk and grabbed her bag for school.

SEAVIEW TERRACE 8:10 A.M.

Alexis Lewis zipped up her jeans and pulled a CMS Bulldogs T-shirt over her head. Now, where was her reporter's notebook? She found it on her desk and dropped the notebook into her backpack. She was covering the pep rally today and the big game between the CMS Bulldogs and the Santa Rosa Cougars next week. The Bulldog-Cougar game was the most important game of the year. And she was the only seventh-grader covering it for the school paper.

The sports rivalry between the two towns had been going on for as long as anyone could remember. The Bulldogs beat the Cougars two years ago, but the Cougars beat the Bulldogs last year and had the big gold trophy to prove it. The Bulldogs desperately wanted that trophy back in their trophy case.

Alexis took a deep breath to calm herself. If I'm this nervous because I have to write this article, she thought, imagine how I'd feel if I'd made the cheerleading squad. Alexis wondered if any of the other girls who didn't make the squad were as relieved as she was not to be a cheerleader. The only bad thing about not being a cheerleader was that Emily, her best friend in the whole world, had made the squad. Emily was so busy with cheerleading practices that they didn't hang out together after school the way they used to.

Alexis had hardly seen Emily over the past two weeks. But she was invited to a sleepover at Emily's tonight. Alexis was glad that this was a Dad week and not a Mom week in her joint custody schedule. Her mother always wanted her home at night. "I only see you half the time," she'd say. "That's bad enough." But her father would let her stay over at Emily's whenever she wanted.

Tonight would be like the good old days — before Emily became a cheerleader.

CLAYMORE MIDDLE SCHOOL. EAST WING. GIRLS' BATHROOM 8:25 A.M.

Sally Johnson studied her reflection in the bathroom mirror. Her uniform finally looked the way she wanted it — with a co-captain's gold star on the skirt. It was so great being co-captain of the cheer squad. What makes it even more perfect, she thought, is that my boyfriend is Darryl Budd, captain of the football team. Sally was sure she was the most popular girl in the school now. Mae Lee, the other co-captain, was nowhere near as popular. Mae didn't even seem to care about popularity and was too serious to be fun. And boys love fun-loving girls.

Melody Max emerged from one of the bathroom stalls. Something about that girl irked Sally. For one thing she was too pretty and uppity for a seventh-grader. Be nice to the seventh-graders, Sally reminded herself. You never know who you might need on your side.

Sally exchanged a smile with Melody in the wide mirror over the sinks. "Don't forget to come to the gym during lunch hour," Sally told her. "To help bring the banners out to the field."

"I'll be there," Melody said. She knocked on a stall door. "You okay, Emily? Does it fit?"

"Yup," Emily replied. She opened the door and came out.

"That looks great, Emily," Melody told her.

"I better comb my hair again," Emily said.

The signal for homeroom buzzed over the loudspeaker.

"I have to grab something from my locker before homeroom," Melody told Emily. "Catch you later."

As Sally put on a little lipstick she noticed Emily Granger sneaking glances at her. "This is your first pep rally," Sally said. "You excited?"

"Oh, yes," Emily answered.

"Was there a problem with your uniform?"

Sally asked. "I heard Melody ask you if it fit."

"We mixed up uniforms," Emily said. "We had to switch. But this one's mine." Emily looked in the mirror and tried to shift the waistband so that the pleats were even on both sides. She had to unbutton it to move it around her waist.

"Does that one fit all right?" Sally asked.

"I think so," Emily said. "Does it look all right?"

Sally looked Emily over. Actually her uniform fit fine, but she was the chubbiest girl on the squad. Sally was convinced that the only reason Emily Granger was a CMS cheerleader was because her family was so active in CMS sports. If Emily dropped a little weight, Sally thought, she might cheer better.

"You know," she told Emily, "now that you mention it, it seems a little tight."

"It feels sort of small," Emily admitted.

"Have you been eating a lot?" Sally asked.

Emily blushed. "I guess," she said.

"Maybe you should watch what you eat," Sally suggested. "Go on a diet. That's what I do when I gain a few extra pounds." She flashed Emily a smile. "It's hard, but it's worth it."

"Okay," Emily said. "I will."

Three eighth-graders rushed into the bathroom and came over to the mirror. Sally glanced at her watch. "I have to go to the office. I'm talking about the pep rally over the loudspeaker during homeroom announcements."

Emily followed Sally out to the hall. As Sally bounced down the hallway people smiled and said hi to her. She's so pretty, thought Emily, and she's so thin.

Emily knew that Sally thought she only made the squad because of her family connections. And she knew that other cheerleaders thought the same thing. She would go on a diet, just like Sally said she should. And work harder than ever on her cheerleading moves.

She'd make sure that she deserved her spot on the squad.

CMS GIRLS' LOCKER ROOM 2:00 P.M.

The cheerleaders had left their classes early to warm up and get ready for the pep rally. Soon classes would be dismissed for the day, and everyone in the building would go to the football field. It was the first appearance of the CMS cheerleaders. Sally knew that the new cheerleaders were excited and more than a little nervous. She remembered her first pep rally. I've come a long way, she thought, from nervous seventh-grader to the ninth-grade co-captain of the squad.

Sally's mother was busy helping the girls with a last-minute check on their appearance.

Sally Sue Johnson, the squad mother in charge of uniforms, hair, and makeup, had been a big-deal college cheerleader. She loved cheerleading as much as her daughter Sally did.

"You have the most beautiful skin," Sally heard her mother saying to someone.

Sally went around the last locker in the row and saw her mother applying a light pink gloss to Melody Max's lips. "And Coach tells me you're a smashing cheerleader, Melody," Sally's mother added.

"Careful what you say to her, Sally Sue," Coach Cortes called from the other side of the room. "Don't want her to get a big head."

Melody smiled.

Melody is so smug, thought Sally. Why does everyone think she's so special?

"Well, I'm looking forward to seeing you cheer," Mrs. Johnson told Melody. "Bend your head. I'll put sparkles in your hair."

Sally caught her mother's eye. "Is my lipstick okay, Mom?" she asked.

"Ah, honey," Sally Sue said. "You look perfectly marvelous. And I just love seeing that gold star on your skirt."

"Thanks, Mom," Sally said.

Coach Cortes shouted, "Okay, everybody, line up. We're going out there."

Emily's heart jumped in her chest. It was time

to perform at her first pep rally. The band was already on the field playing the school fight song. Even her snug waistband didn't matter now. She was a *cheerleader*. She had a job to do. She fell in line behind Melody and ran out onto the field.

"And here they are — your classmates and cheerleaders — the CMS Cheer Squad!" the athletic director shouted over the field's sound system.

Joan looked at the crowd in the bleachers, threw a fist in the air to salute them, and did three handsprings in a row. Out of the corner of her eye she saw the rest of the squad running, jumping, and tumbling. On a signal from Sally they all fell into line in front of the crowd. It was time for their first sideline chant. Sally raised the megaphone to her lips and shouted:

We're here. X X (clap, clap)
Let's cheer. X X

Next they led the crowd in a color chant for blue and white. Then they did a competition cheer to see which grade could yell loudest — seventh, eighth, or ninth. By now the crowd was heated up, and it was time to introduce the football team. The cheerleaders picked up their pom-poms and ran toward the entrance of the field. They faced one another in two rows and raised their arms to make an arch of blue-and-white pom-poms.

As each football player's name was announced, the player — in full uniform — ran under the human arch onto the field. The last player to come out had Bubba IV with him. Bubba had on his uniform, too — an extra-small CMS T-shirt and a blue leather collar with silver spikes. The crowd cheered for Bubba as he waddled onto the field and stood in front of the line of players.

Someone in the bleachers stood up and yelled, "Kill the Cougars!"

A few kids laughed, but others picked up the chant, stamping their feet and yelling, "Kill the Cougars!"

It was time for the national anthem and the pledge. Emily looked around to see what they should do. Sally gave the signal to break the arch formation, and the cheerleaders ran to the middle of the field in a line beside the football players.

The crowd quieted down, and everyone stood while the band played "America the Beautiful." Next, everyone said the Pledge of Allegiance.

Then the band played the school fight song, and the cheerleaders led the singing. They were determined to keep the crowd pepped up. At the end of the song the cheerleaders did tumbles and jumps and ran off the field. It was time for the principal and the coach to make speeches.

As Melody ran off the field, Darryl Budd, the CMS quarterback, gave her a thumbs-up sign. Melody loved it. The captain and star of the football team was telling *her* she was great.

Sally, who was already at the sidelines, noticed Darryl's thumbs-up sign and saw Melody's pleased reaction. Sally made sure to catch Darryl's eye and flashed him her best smile. He smiled back, and from the corner of her eye Sally watched Melody's smile fade.

Sally's thoughts of Darryl and Melody were interrupted by a low growl. She looked down. Bubba was standing next to her. What an ugly dog, she thought. Coach Cortes once said, "Bubba is so ugly that he's cute. That pup has the sweetest disposition."

Sweet? thought Sally. Are you kidding me? She hated that dog. She felt like kicking him all the time. She would have, too, if hundreds of people weren't there watching and she wasn't so afraid of the dribbling little monster.

Bubba growled up at her again. Sally looked around. People could see her, but they couldn't hear her over the band music. She leaned over, put on a fake smile, and said between her teeth, "Get away from me, you flat-faced little creep."

Bubba didn't budge. He glared at her and bared *his* teeth.

Sally backed away and listened to what the principal, Mr. Asche, was saying.

"Our rivalry with Santa Rosa is intense," he said. "Things happened at the game last year that are best put behind us. I expect all of you — fans, players, cheerleaders — to represent the best in CMS with good sportsmanship and spirit."

Put last year behind us? thought Sally. No way. The game was at Santa Rosa. CMS lost. The Bulldog players said that the Cougars played dirty. To make matters worse, their cheerleaders had been rude to the Bulldog cheer squad. Whenever the Bulldog cheerleaders led a chant or did a cheer, the Cougar fans shouted over them. And during halftime the Cougar band played so that the Bulldog cheerleaders couldn't do their halftime routine. The Cougar cheerleaders didn't even try to control the crowd.

But what bothered Sally more was that Cougar cheerleaders placed at the CHEER USA competitions in Miami and the Bulldog squad did not. All because one of last year's flyers fell twice. It was all Allison's fault. Well, Allison was in high school now, and the Bulldogs had Joan. We're going to place in Miami this year, thought Sally. And starting at the game next week the Cougar cheerleaders are going to know which squad is on top.

Emily, looking up from the sidelines, noticed her mother and Lily. Lily looked so cute in her cheerleading outfit. Then Emily saw Jake and Alexis sitting together on the top bleacher. Emily waved. She loved that her two best friends in the world were sitting together.

Since Jake was the editor of the school paper, the *Bulldog Edition*, he was Alexis's boss. But Alexis didn't mind. She'd always looked up to Jake, ever since she and Emily had become best friends in first grade and she started hanging out at the Grangers'.

Jake's parents and younger sister had died in a fire when he was five years old. Since that awful accident, he lived with his grandparents in a house right behind the Grangers' home and business, The Manor Hotel. Emily was the same age as Jake's sister would have been. He was especially close to Emily and practically a member of the Granger family.

"There are a lot of adults here," Jake told Alexis. "I've never seen so many people show up for a pep rally or get so worked up over a game."

"I was thinking of interviewing Darryl for the article," Alexis said. "I'd ask him, 'What does the captain of the football team think of the rivalry with the Cougars and what happened at the game last year?' "

"Good idea," Jake said.

The cheerleaders ran out to the center of the field to do their big number. They did a three-minute routine that included tumbling, a dance, and stunts. It ended with Joan and Sally being held at the top of a team stunt pyramid.

Alexis smiled at her friends on the squad. The CMS cheerleaders looked great. The crowd was excited and ready for the Cougars. She just hoped she was ready to be a *Bulldog Edition* reporter.

THE MANOR HOTEL.
BULLDOG CAFÉ 5:00 P.M.

Emily stood in the middle of the outdoor café. It was mobbed with football players and cheerleaders. There was plenty of soda and juice in a big cooler, and Jake and a couple of players were grilling hot dogs and burgers. As people on the street walked by, they stopped to encourage the players. Everyone was having a great time.

Jake came over with a couple of hot dogs and handed one to Emily. "I'm taking a break from the grill," he said. He smiled at her. "Hey, you looked great out there today, Em."

"Thanks," she said, taking a bite of the hot dog. They stood there side by side, talking about the big game and eating. Emily had already had a burger, but she was still famished. She was halfway through the hot dog when she looked up and saw Sally looking at her.

Emily felt embarrassed. Sally said she should go on a diet, and here she was, stuffing her face again. I have to stop eating so much, she thought. But not tonight. Tonight's a party. Tomorrow I'll start my diet.

Sally wasn't thinking about Emily eating. She was looking for Darryl. Her main objective at this party was to keep her boyfriend away from Melody. But where was Darryl? Sally finally saw him, walking across the deck with two sodas. He was headed toward Melody, who stood talking and laughing with Joan and her brother, Adam.

Sally moved quickly and reached the group an instant before Darryl did. "Hey, guys," she said. "How's it going?"

Darryl came up to them, looked from Melody to Sally, and then looked down at the two sodas. He handed one soda to Sally and the other to Melody.

Melody liked that Darryl brought her a soda, but she didn't believe he was interested in her. Why would he be when he had Sally Johnson, beautiful co-captain of the cheer squad and president of the ninth-grade class, for a girlfriend?

Before Sally could figure out a way to get

Darryl away from Melody, Alexis joined them.

"Darryl," she said. "I'm writing an article about the pep rally and game for the *Bulldog Edition*. I'd love to interview you for it."

Darryl grinned. "We're going to destroy the Cougars," he said. "Write that."

"Okay," she said. "But I also have a bunch of questions I want to ask you. Maybe we could go to the lobby, where it's not so noisy. Do you mind?"

"Nah, I don't mind," Darryl said. "Just as long as you start with how we're gonna kill 'em."

"Have you seen Jake?" Sally asked Alexis, even though she knew exactly where he was.

"He's working the barbecue grill," Alexis told her.

"What a guy," said Sally. "Always doing something nice for people. That's what I love about him."

Sally caught the crushed look on Darryl's face before she turned and headed across the deck toward Jake. Good, she thought. It won't hurt to make him think I might like Jake.

In the lobby, Alexis sat on the edge of an easy chair facing Darryl, who sat on the couch. She loved doing the interview with Darryl, but she was surprised at how hostile he was toward the Cougars. "They play dirty," he said, leaning forward. He ground a fist into his palm. "But we're going to teach them a lesson. We're getting that trophy back."

When Alexis finished the interview with Darryl she went back out to the deck. People were starting to leave. Sally was still there, sitting at one of the tables and having a soda with Jake. Alexis wanted to tell Jake about the interview with Darryl. But Jake was busy talking to Sally. Alexis felt funny walking over to them so she looked for her friends. She saw Joan cleaning up.

Joan was throwing empty cans into a recycling bag when she heard a horn honk three times. Joan looked to the street. "My mother," she told Alexis. She turned to Emily, who was clearing away plates from a table. "I have to go. Thanks for the party."

"I wish you could sleep over," Emily said.

"Another time," Joan told her.

" 'Bye, Joan," Melody called.

As Joan waved good-bye to her friends, she wondered when she'd ever be able to go to a sleepover at a friend's house. Would Emily eventually stop asking her?

When Joan reached the car Adam was standing beside it, talking to their mother through the window. "I'll be in by eleven," Adam said as he opened the car door for Joan. At that moment Joan hated her brother. He could stay out until eleven, but she couldn't stay for Emily's sleepover. She glared at him, got in the car, and reached over to close the door herself.

Joan wanted to tell her parents that she felt as old as Adam. She and Adam were both in middle school, even if he was an eighth-grader and she was a seventh-grader. But her parents had a strict set of rules for raising their children. One rule was, "You don't argue with your mother or father." Another one seemed to be, "Adam will always have more freedom than Joanie."

As the car pulled away from The Manor Hotel, Joan turned and looked out the back window.

Emily and Melody were sitting at one of the tables with Emily's little sister. They were laughing about something that Lily was saying.

Darryl and Sally were walking arm in arm down the street. A whole crowd of ninth-graders were bunched behind them. Adam was one of them, the creep.

Jake and Alexis were standing on the sidewalk in front of the café, talking animatedly.

And here I am, Joan thought, going home with my mother.

She couldn't wait until she graduated from high school and could do whatever she wanted.

THE MANOR HOTEL 11:00 P.M.

Alexis lay across Emily's bed. Emily and Melody sat on the floor in front of the TV. They were watching a videotape of last year's CHEER USA competitions in Miami. I'd rather watch a basketball game, thought Alexis. But Melody and Emily loved watching the cheerleading competitions. This was the third time they'd run the tape.

Melody handed Alexis the bowl of chips. "Miami is such a great place," she said. "You guys have got to come when I go visit my dad sometime."

"We'll be in Miami for the CHEER USA competition," said Emily.

"It'll be so much fun," said Melody. "I'll introduce you all to my Miami friends. Really, Miami is so cool. There's this great hip-hop club we can go to."

Emily pointed the remote at the VCR and froze the image on the TV screen. "Look at that flyer!" she shouted. "Check out that basket toss! Joan has to see this tape. I'll lend it to her." Emily pressed the play button, and the flyer landed in the arms of the bases below her. Emily took a handful of chips.

"I don't think Joan has a TV and VCR," Melody said. "Her parents won't allow it. But she and Adam are coming over to swim tomorrow. You should come, too. Bring the tape and Joan can watch it."

"Okay," said Emily.

"You, too, Alexis," Melody added. "It'll be a pool party. Very Miami."

"I can't," Alexis said. "I'm having lunch with my father and my aunt Louise, then I have to work on the article for the school paper." Alexis also wanted to play some basketball Sunday afternoon. She wished she'd spent all the hours she'd practiced for the cheerleading tryouts shooting baskets. It would have been a lot more fun, she thought.

When the tape ended, Emily flipped over on her side and looked at her friends. "What do you want to do now?" she asked. "We could go downstairs and have some ice cream."

"I'm not hungry," Alexis said. "But I'm really tired."

"Me, too," Melody said with a yawn.

"I'll take the sleeping bag, Melody," Alexis offered. "You can sleep in the extra bed."

"I don't mind sleeping on the floor," Melody said.

While Melody and Alexis discussed who was going to sleep where, Emily gathered up the snack dishes and empty glasses and left for the kitchen. It was eleven-thirty. In a half hour her diet would officially begin.

There was time for one last dish of ice cream.

DOLPHIN COURT APARTMENTS.
POOLSIDE. SATURDAY 3:00 P.M.

Every time Emily was tempted by the snacks Melody put out, she peered down at her stomach. It was like a big soft mound sitting on her lap. Melody has a totally flat stomach, thought Emily, even when she sits down. Joan — who had just left for her piano lesson — was even skinnier than Melody, and she was *always* eating. It's not fair, Emily thought.

Emily's stomach rumbled with hunger. All she'd eaten so far that day was a small bowl of cereal with skim milk. I'll be as thin as they are, she vowed to herself. I *have* to be, or I won't be a good cheerleader, and we won't place at CHEER USA.

Melody and Adam were splashing around in the water, throwing a ball back and forth.

"Come on in, Emily," Melody shouted.

"Later," Emily shouted back. "I'll come in later."

Emily sat back in a lounge chair and closed her eyes. She could hear Melody and Adam comparing bands and singers they liked as they tossed the ball back and forth. They hummed lines of music, recited lyrics, and laughed a lot.

Emily wondered what Jake was doing. She held her wrist in front of her face and squinted at her watch. Three o'clock. He was just getting off work. He'll probably go home and do his homework, she thought. Maybe he and his grandparents will have dinner with us tonight. Saturday night dinner in the hotel dining room was a Granger family tradition. The Feders often joined them.

Dinner, thought Emily. She imagined the pink tablecloth covered with heaps of delicious food. A basket of hot homemade rolls, fried shrimp with dipping sauce, roast chicken, rice, beans, and salad. Then the dessert wagon would be pushed over to their table. Her mouth watered, she felt so hungry!

She wished she could hate eating as much as she hated dieting.

DOLPHIN COURT APARTMENTS.
SUNDAY 11:45 A.M.

Melody Max went on-line to check her e-mail. There were messages from Miami from Tina and Jackie. They were full of news about her old gang and the dance class Melody had been in with them. The piece of news that surprised Melody most was that Juan Ramirez, the hottest guy in the school, was asking about her. Melody didn't know if Juan, who never used to pay any attention to her, was really interested in her or if it was a figment of boy-crazy Tina's imagination. Tina ended the e-mail with a question.

> So fess up, Max, how dorky are the guys in
> Boremore? Tell all or you will not hear an-
> other word from me. I mean I'll be mean.
> Love ya, but not if you don't answer the
> question. The Big T.

Melody was picturing Big T as she'd last seen her, waving good-bye from the sidewalk when Melody and her mother drove away on moving day. Tina was the smallest of Melody's Miami friends. Her nickname was a joke. And the idea of Big T being *mean* was an even bigger joke.

Melody checked her watch. If she was quick about it she could type an answer to Tina's letter before she went out to dinner with her mother and two of her mother's new friends from the paper. If Big T wanted to hear about guys, she'd tell her about guys.

> Big T: How nosy are you? Well, listen up, be-
> cause I have some guy news for you. Clay-
> more is Boremore no more. The guys are
> a-okay. Let me tell you about these guys —
> three of them anyway — who are becoming
> friends. Two of them are ninth-graders and

the other one is in the eighth grade. You're dying to hear about them, right? First there's Darryl, ninth-grader, football captain, and major hunk. Would like to be better pals with him, but he's got this glory blond cheer captain gal on his arm, which he likes plenty good enough. Darryl's always making eye contact with me of the "Aren't you cute? Aren't I cute?" variety. I suspect he's a bit dim and not in on how complicated Girl Power can be. Next, there's Jake Feder, also in the ninth grade. Now, Jake is what you'd call an all-around smart sweetie pie. Jake's down-to-earth with a golden heart. Good to be around and no snob. Spending time with seventh-graders no prob for him. Last is Adam. Yup. He's the eighth-grader. Adam's sister, Joan, a good friend, is on the cheer squad with me. Adam is the coolest of the guys I've met here — in my terms. He makes me laugh, which is way important on my friendship meter. Adam knows loads about music, even hip-hop, though he's never been to a live concert that wasn't classical music. He has strict-beyond-belief parents. This parent thing is a major prob, but he takes it on and doesn't much complain, which makes him a lot different from Melody-the-Whiner. (Remember when I first moved here and all I did was complain?)

The girls I hang with aren't pairing off with guys. I'm glad. It's so much fun when a big group of guys and girls are hanging together and just being friends. Don't you think? Or are you all gaga over some big dude I would not approve of? Do tell or I'll be mean. Love ya. The Max.:-)

As Melody was signing off on her e-mail she heard the other phone line ring and her mother answer it.

"Melody, it's for you," her mother called.

"Who is it?" Melody called back.

"A boy. Darryl," her mother answered as she opened the door. "Be quick, Mel. We're already late for dinner."

Melody picked up the phone in her room. Why was Darryl calling *her*?

After they both said *Hi* and *How are you?* they talked about the pep rally. He told her she was a good cheerleader and that she would probably be a co-captain when she was in the ninth grade. She thanked him for encouraging her to try out for cheering in the first place. He said again that he could tell she was a good dancer and asked her how old she was.

"Twelve," she answered.

"Oh," he said. "I thought maybe you were older."

"Nope," she said. "I'm twelve for real."

She didn't know what else to say, so she asked him if he liked hip-hop. He said he hadn't heard much hip-hop but would be interested in learning more about it. She promised to lend him a CD.

"Melody," her mother called. "Let's go."

"I have to go," Melody told Darryl.

When she'd hung up she wondered why he had called her. Then she remembered the question, "How old are you?" That must be why he called, she thought. Maybe he hoped that I was older than I am. Maybe if I was older he'd want to go out with me.

She had had crushes on older guys when she was in sixth grade. But none of them showed any interest in her. If I was thirteen would Darryl Budd ask me on a date? she wondered. Maybe he would ask her out anyway. Did she want him to? Melody tried to imagine herself as Darryl's date. What would it be like to be the girlfriend of just about the most popular guy in school?

Well, for now, only Sally Johnson knew the answer to that question.

DELHAVEN DRIVE 7:30 P.M.

Joan was washing the dinner dishes, and her mother was wiping them. Adam and her father had cooked dinner, so it was Joan and her mother's turn to clean up. Joan wanted to ask her mother why they couldn't have a dishwasher like other people. But she knew the answer. Her parents were against anything that had anything to do with high technology. Joan could argue that there wasn't much high-tech about a dishwasher — that it was a rather simple machine that had been around for more than fifty years. If I argued with my parents about everything we disagree about, she thought, all we would do is argue.

Her mother was asking Joan about the readings in her English literature class when the phone rang. At least we have a phone, Joan thought as her mother went to answer it. It's not a portable, and there's only one in the whole house — but it's certainly better than smoke signals for communication.

Joan listened to see if the call was for her. If it was, she knew that her mother would say that she was busy and that Joan would call back later. Or she might say, "Joanie will see you in school tomorrow." But the phone call wasn't for her. It was *about* her. From her piano teacher.

When Joan's mother hung up, she put down the towel and said in a low, serious tone, "I have to speak to your father."

Joan knew they would be speaking about her.

Then there would be a joint assault from her parents about her piano lessons.

She was right. They were waiting for her when she left the kitchen a few minutes later.

"Sit down, Joanie," her father said. "We want to speak to you about your piano lessons."

She sat on the edge of the easy chair, and her parents sat side by side on the couch facing her. Two against one.

"First," her mother began. "You asked to change your Saturday piano lesson to Thursday after school, and Mr. Richter accommodated you."

"Because of cheering for games," Joan said. "You said that was okay."

"It is," said her father. "But what isn't okay is that Mr. Richter says that your playing is not improving at any appreciable rate. He questions whether you've slacked off on your practice sessions. Have you?"

"I practice for half an hour every night," Joan told them.

"What happened to the hour you used to practice?" her father asked.

"That was when I was in elementary school," Joan said. "I have more homework in middle school." Her heart pounded. She was afraid of what they would say next.

"You should come directly home after

school," her mother said. "That way you can practice piano for an hour and still have plenty of time for your homework."

But I have cheerleading practice three days a week after school, Joan thought. When football season started there would be after-school games in addition to weekend games. As a cheerleader she was expected to attend all practices and games. If she was absent more than twice she would be cut from the squad. She didn't say any of this to her parents. Instead, she said, "But there are extracurricular activities after school. Like debate club. You wanted me to join that."

Joan felt her throat tighten the way it did whenever she lied to her parents. She hated lying. She'd only been doing it since she started middle school and decided to try out for cheerleading. When she went to cheer clinics she had told her parents that she was attending debate club meetings. Even after her mother signed the permission slip for her to be a cheerleader, she didn't tell them that she hadn't joined the debate club.

"Maybe this cheerleading business is taking up too much of your time," her father suggested.

"Adam doesn't have to be home till six o'clock," she tried. "And don't say he's older, because that was the rule when he was in seventh grade, too. I remember."

"We didn't have a phone call from his violin teacher," her mother said.

Don't be afraid, Joan told herself. Don't act like a brat. And don't act like a baby. She took a deep breath.

"Please," she said, "give me another chance. I'll be home by five at the latest. I promise I'll practice an hour every day, even on weekends. I love playing piano." That wasn't a lie. She did love playing the piano. "And I love cheerleading. I won't hang out with my friends after my extra-curricular activities. I'll come right home. By five."

Her father whispered something in her mother's ear. They looked at each other and nodded.

"Okay," her father said. "We'll have a two-week trial period. If your piano playing improves you may remain in the debate club and on the cheer team."

Joan didn't bother to tell her father that it was called a cheer squad. The less her parents knew about cheerleading, the better.

"Thank you," she said.

The phone rang again. Joan jumped up. "I'll get it," she said. She ran into the kitchen. This time it was for her. Emily wanted to know what they had for math homework. She also asked Joan what she'd had for dinner. "Spaghetti with meatballs and garlic bread," Joan told her. "Oh, yeah, and a salad. Adam makes great salad dressing."

"Did you have dessert?" Emily asked.

Joan said her parents didn't like desserts that much, but that she liked them. She told Emily she was lucky to have her own café and restaurant. That it must be fun to live in a hotel. Joan loved having a chatty phone call with one of her friends, but she knew her parents didn't approve of long phone conversations. So she signed off pretty quickly and went into the living room to practice the piano.

As she opened her sheet music and put it on the piano, Joan was still thinking about cheerleading. But once she began to play, her mind focused on the music. It was a piece by Beethoven that expressed anxiety and joy. This music sounds the way I feel, thought Joan. She played it with all her heart.

CMS COURTYARD. MONDAY 8:20 A.M.

It was a Mom week, so Alexis's mother gave her a ride to school. As Mrs. Lewis pulled the car up in front of CMS she was talking about what they would have for dinner. Alexis only half heard her. She was distracted by a big crowd of kids gathered in the school courtyard. It wasn't unusual for kids to be in the courtyard of the

U-shaped building before school. But usually they were in small groups scattered around the space. This morning they were all bunched together facing the front door.

"Whatever you want for dinner is fine with me," Alexis told her mother as she jumped out of the car. She closed the door and ran to the courtyard. As she approached the crowd she heard kids saying, "That's disgusting." And, "I hate the Cougars." And, "It's *so* horrible!"

Alexis tried to look past the heads of the kids in front of her. Finally she saw what everyone was looking at. A dog was hanging by its neck over the front doors of the building. It looked like Bubba. It *was* Bubba.

She screamed.

"It's a stuffed animal," she heard someone say. She turned to see Jake standing next to her. He put a hand on her elbow. "It's not real."

"The Cougars?" asked Alexis.

Jake nodded.

The life-size stuffed Bubba swung from a rope that was tied around its neck, hangman style. Even though Alexis knew it wasn't real it looked so much like Bubba it gave her chills. On the door behind the Bubba effigy were large spray-painted letters in red and black that read COUGARS WILL WIN!

"Where's Emily?" Alexis asked.

38

"With the other cheerleaders," Jake said, pointing to the front steps of the school.

The cheerleaders stood facing the crowd. Darryl and some other guys Alexis recognized from the football team were there, too.

Sally came forward with the megaphone and yelled, **"Fight, Bulldogs, FIGHT!"**

The crowd picked up the chant. The football players threw fists in the air and helped lead the crowd. Sally handed the megaphone to Mae, who continued to shout the familiar chant. Meanwhile, a group of cheerleaders held Sally up in an extension so she could reach the stuffed Bubba. She untied the cord around his neck, and he fell into the waiting arms of another cheerleader. Alexis saw that it was Emily.

Emily looked down at the Bubba effigy. It looked so much like her Bubba that she thought she was going to throw up. If I had eaten breakfast, she thought, I'd be losing it right now.

Just then a loud buzzer sounded over the courtyard loudspeaker. It was the CMS signal for immediate silence and attention. Mae gave a signal for the cheerleaders to stop chanting. They did. But some of the football players and the crowd kept chanting **"Fight, Bulldogs, Fight!"** without them. Emily noticed that some teachers were trying to quiet the group down.

The front doors opened, splitting the word COUGARS between the G and the A. The principal, Mr. Asche, came out. He put a hand on Darryl's arm. Darryl saw who it was and stopped chanting. Mr. Asche said something to Darryl. Darryl nodded, raised the megaphone to his mouth, and said in a booming voice, "Listen up! Mr. Asche wants to talk."

There was still an echo of **"Get the Cougars!"** as some in the crowd continued to chant.

"I MEAN IT!" Darryl shouted.

Finally, the crowd quieted down and Mr. Asche spoke. He said that he would be placing a call to the principal of Santa Rosa Middle School. He added that he was depending on the football players, the cheerleaders, the students of CMS, and the citizens of Claymore to behave with more dignity than the people who had defaced the CMS mascot and school building.

A few kids booed, but most of the kids were silent and waited to see what Mr. Asche would do next. CMS was a pretty strict school. A person could be suspended for booing the principal.

When the boos died down, Mr. Asche spoke in a calm, level voice, but you could hear the anger underneath. "Students, go to your homerooms."

The principal stepped aside, and the kids

started moving into the school building. Some of them gently touched the Bubba effigy in Emily's arms as they passed her. One of them said, "Sorry, Emily."

Coach Cortes came over to her. "Why don't I take that to my office?" she said.

"It looks just like Bubba," Emily said as she handed over the stuffed animal.

"I know," said Coach. "I had a fright when I first saw it."

"Me, too," Emily told her as they walked into the building together.

Melody, Alexis, and Joan met her in the front lobby, and the four friends headed for their lockers. The talking in the lobby and corridors was louder than usual.

"Someone has to teach them a lesson they won't forget," one girl said to another as they passed Emily.

"We can't let them get away with this," she overheard a tall, dark-haired boy tell a small group of ninth-graders who had gathered around him.

As Emily looked around, she noticed everyone was talking about the Cougars.

During homeroom, Mr. Asche spoke to the student body over the public address system. He reported that the principal of Santa Rosa Middle School, Ms. Hylton, apologized for the vandalism. She and Mr. Asche suspected that high school kids from Santa Rosa may have been involved. Ms. Hylton intended to find out who was responsible. Mr. Asche said he had assured Ms. Hylton that there would be no retaliation from members of the CMS student body. He instructed his students to spread the word in town that CMS would practice good sportsmanship. He expected the cheerleaders and football squad to set the example for the rest of the school.

Emily took a deep breath. She hoped that everything would be all right.

CMS SMALL GYM 3:30 P.M.

When the cheerleaders came into the gym they were all still talking about the desecration of their mascot and the graffiti on the school doors.

Coach Cortes was waiting for them. "Take your warm-up positions," she announced in a stern voice.

The talking quickly died down as the cheerleaders went to their positions.

As soon as everyone was ready Coach spoke. "I've seen and heard what's been going on in this school today," she began, "and there's too much anger going down. It's our job to turn it around. How many of you can stay for an extra hour after practice to make some posters? I want a positive message in the halls this week. Who can I count on?"

Joan put her hand up and looked around. Everyone's hand was up. All the cheerleaders were going to pitch in and make posters. Everyone but me, Joan suddenly thought. I have to be home by five to practice piano. She put her hand down. She felt like a baby.

Emily felt her stomach rumble. She'd had an upset stomach all day — ever since she first saw the effigy and thought that it was her dog. It was a perfect replica of Bubba, down to the brown tip on his right ear. Whoever made it knew exactly what Bubba looked like.

"Okay," Coach said. "Now let's talk about how we are going to conduct ourselves next week when the Cougars are here. Any ideas?"

"Maybe we shouldn't let them do a center cheer," C.J., one of the ninth-grade cheerleaders, yelled out. "They didn't let us do one when we were on their field last year. Remember?"

"And they chanted over our chants," Kelly added.

Someone called out, "They weren't fair."

Another girl shouted, "Let's treat them the way they treated us."

Coach put up her hand. "Sorry, gang," she

said. "That wasn't the right answer, and I think you know it. Try again."

Sally stepped forward. "It's our responsibility to keep the spirit of sportsmanship alive at every game," she said. "We'll be courteous to the Cougar cheerleaders. We'll give them equal time in the center field. And we won't interrupt their chants."

Coach applauded. The cheerleaders joined in. Sally grinned.

Emily clapped the loudest. Sally's so cool, she thought. I wish I could be just like her. I wish I could look just like her.

"I couldn't say it better, Sally," Coach said. "Did you all hear that?"

"Yes," the cheerleaders shouted.

Maria raised her hand. "But Coach, what they did to Bubba . . ."

"I know," Coach said.

"Only a few people are responsible for that," Mae said. "We shouldn't do anything mean back to them. Two wrongs don't make a right."

Melody raised her hand. "I thought of something we can do with the bulldog they strung up," she said. "We can dress it up in CMS gear and put it in the trophy case."

Everyone applauded again.

As she clapped, Sally thought, they're all falling for this goody-goody business. Santa

Rosa wouldn't get away with this. Not if she could help it.

MAIN STREET 6:15 P.M.

Emily was walking home along Main Street, chanting over and over in her head, *I'm so hungry. I'm so hungry.* That's not going to help me stay on this diet, she told herself. She changed the chant to, *I'm so fat. I'm so fat.* She was going back and forth between *I'm so hungry* and *I'm so fat* as she approached Bulldog Café.

Jake was there with his grandparents. Her father had pulled a chair up to visit with them, and Bubba lay at his feet. He saw Emily and motioned for her to come over. Bubba waddled over to meet her. When they met, Emily squatted and Bubba put his front legs on her thighs. She gave her real-life dog a big hug and carried him over to her father and the Feders.

When Emily sat down, Mrs. Feder said, "Tell us your version of what happened today, dear."

Emily told them how at first she thought it was their actual dog hanging from the rope. Then she reported that the cheerleaders made posters to keep school spirit headed in the right direction and that the stuffed bulldog now sat in the trophy case dressed in a CMS T-shirt and baseball cap. "He's holding a little sign that says 'CMS. We're the best!' " she added.

45

While Emily spoke she checked out what Jake and his grandparents were eating. Jake had a chicken burrito. She loved the salsa and guacamole that came with that dish. Mrs. Feder was eating a turkey club sandwich — a Bulldog Café specialty and one of Emily's favorite things to eat in the whole world. Mr. Feder was eating an enormous half chicken with french fries.

Emily wondered, How come they're not fat and I am?

Jake's grandmother, who was principal of the Claymore High School, said that the Cougar prank was being talked about all over her school, too. She made an announcement similar to the one Mr. Asche had made in the middle school. "I told them that there was to be no act of retaliation against the Cougars. That the mischief has to stop now before the pranks become meaner and more dangerous. Anyone in my school who becomes involved will be looking at a suspension."

"We have to try to keep a lid on this thing," Jake's grandfather added, "or someone will be hurt."

"A lot of people stopped by the hotel to talk about it today," Emily's father said. "You must have been pretty shocked, honey." He tapped Emily on the arm. "Emily, are you listening to me?"

She reluctantly looked away from the food on the table and at her father. "Yeah," she said. "It was pretty awful."

"Why don't you pull up a chair and eat something?" her father said.

"You look tired, Emily," Mrs. Feder said. "Sit here next to me. You can start by sharing my sandwich while the kitchen makes your meal."

Jake got a chair for Emily from one of the other tables. Before she knew what she was doing she was sitting between Jake and his grandmother and biting into a turkey club sandwich. Her father asked her what she wanted to order. She swallowed the bite in her mouth. "Another turkey club," she answered. She smiled at Mrs. Feder. "We'll split it."

"And let's have some sweet potato fries," Mrs. Feder said. "We both like those."

Emily nodded. "I'll have a mixed fruit smoothie, too," she told her father as he stood up to place the order. Emily smiled as she took another bite.

She couldn't believe how good that sandwich tasted.

CMS LOBBY. TUESDAY 8:25 A.M.

Joan, walking through the lobby, thought that the posters the other cheerleaders made were great. She just wished that she had been able to

47

help. Her favorite had a big football spiraling though a blue sky. Big white lettering read:

CMS FOOTBALL HAS THE SPIN.
WE PLAY HARD.
WE PLAY FAIR.
WE WIN!

The other posters in the lobby had positive messages, too.

Melody came up behind her. "Did you see Bubba?" she asked.

"Is Bubba here?" Joan asked with surprise. "In school?"

"Not the real one," Melody answered. She pointed to the trophy case. "Look over there."

Joan joined a crowd of kids in front of the glass case. She stood on her tiptoes and saw the cleaned-up, dressed-up Bubba.

"That's great," Joan told Melody.

"Who did it?" someone asked.

"Melody Max," a boy said in a loud voice. Joan looked up and saw Darryl.

Someone in the group of kids said, "Great idea." Someone else said, "Who's Melody Max?" A few kids turned to check out Melody.

Darryl put an arm around Melody's shoulder, whispered something in her ear, and left.

As Joan and Melody walked to their lockers

Joan noticed that Melody looked upset.

"What'd Darryl say to you?" she asked.

"That there are high school kids who will take care of the Cougars," she answered.

"Did he say what they're going to do?" asked Joan.

Melody shook her head. "But it sounds serious. He said, 'They're going to take care of them.' "

"Uh-oh," said Joan. "Should we do something? I mean to stop them."

"I think we should try," Melody answered. "But what can we do?"

"Let's find Emily and Alexis and tell them," Joan said.

"We should have some kind of meeting about this," added Melody.

BULLDOG CAFÉ 4:00 P.M.

Alexis, Melody, and Joan picked out a table where no one could overhear them, while Emily went to the kitchen to get them all lemonade. As she was coming back with the tray of drinks and a plate of chocolate chip cookies, she saw Jake and Adam walking down the street together. The girls at the table saw them, too. Alexis signaled the boys to join them.

Joan came over to help Emily with the drinks. "Alexis thinks that Jake and Adam should be at the meeting," she said.

"Great," said Emily. She held out the tray. "You take this. I'll get them some lemonade."

When Emily joined the meeting Alexis was saying, "Pranks can be fun. The people in my dad's law office are always playing tricks on one another. But it's because they're friends. They'd never do anything really mean."

"Hanging a model of our mascot by the neck is pretty mean," said Jake.

"And not letting our cheerleaders do their center cheer last year," said Joan. "It wasn't a prank. But it was mean."

"I was at that game," Emily told them. "When their cheerleaders kept trying to shout our cheerleaders down, it made our side really angry."

"When I was in Miami," Melody said, "there was this story my mother wrote. It was *bad*. Not the article. What happened. Some fraternity guys at the university threw a can of homemade tear gas through another fraternity house's window. It was awful stuff. The guys who were in that building said their eyes burned for a really long time. But what was worse was that one of the guys died! He had some kind of allergic reaction to whatever they use to make the tear gas."

"Wow!" Jake exclaimed.

"That is out of hand," said Adam.

"What are we going to do to stop whoever it is from doing whatever they're planning to do?" asked Melody.

"First, we have to find out who it is," said Emily.

"And what they're planning to do," added Alexis.

"How?" asked Joan.

"We need to do some major sleuthing," said Alexis.

"My dad might be able to find out something," Emily suggested. "People are always dropping by the hotel and talking to him about CMS sports. I'll ask him to help."

"I'll tell my grandmother what Darryl told Melody," Jake said. "Maybe she can learn more from the kids at her school."

"Don't tell anyone that Darryl is involved," Melody said. "I don't want to get him in trouble."

"Okay," agreed Jake.

"Darryl likes you, Melody," Joan said. "Maybe you could get some more information from him." Joan noticed her brother look at Melody. Does Adam like Melody, too? she wondered. She wished that her brother wasn't at this meeting. These were her friends. Wasn't it bad enough that he had more freedom than she did? Was he going to steal her friends, too? It wasn't fair that

51

she had to be home by five o'clock and he didn't have to be there until six. She looked at her watch. It was already 4:45. She had to get home. Adam could stay, but she'd have to go. She stood up. "I have to go," she told everyone.

"How come?" asked Emily.

Joan didn't want her friends to know that her parents kept her on a short leash. "I have a piano lesson," she said. She gave her brother a quick glance that said, Don't say anything. He didn't.

"You didn't eat your cookie," Emily told her. Emily wondered how Joan could resist the gorgeous cookie on the napkin in front of her. It was taking every bit of willpower that Emily had not to gobble it up.

"You have it," Joan told her. "I'm not hungry. Have to run."

After Joan left, Adam said, "Even if we knew who it was that was going to retaliate, how would we stop them?"

"Good question," said Alexis. "I guess we'll just have to figure that out. Meanwhile, I'll rewrite my sports column. I'll say that the only way CMS is going to get back at the Cougars is by winning that football game."

"And I'll write an editorial," Jake said. "I'll ask everyone to support our decision, as a school, not to try to get back at the Cougars in any other way than by winning the game."

"When is the paper coming out?" Emily asked.

"Friday morning," Jake answered.

"The cheerleaders should give out the papers," Melody said. "We can tell everyone to read the sports column and the editorial."

"That is a great idea," Adam told Melody.

"Thanks," she said softly as she returned his smile.

"But how is that going to stop the pranks?" Emily asked. "The high school kids who are planning them probably won't even see our school paper. They read the *Claymore News*. That's the paper that covers high school sports."

"The *Claymore News* comes out on Friday, too," Melody said. "Maybe my mother will print Alexis's column and Jake's editorial on the sports page. Then a lot of the high school kids will read them, too. I'll ask her tonight."

"Our articles in the town paper?" said Alexis.

"We have to get people to mellow about the Cougars," Adam said. "The papers are one way to do that."

Alexis felt a wave of panic run through her. Was she good enough? "Jake, you have to help me with mine," she said.

"Don't worry," he told her. "The piece you did on the cheer tryouts was really good. This one will be even better."

"Do you think we should ask Sally to talk to Darryl about it?" asked Emily.

"Sally and Darryl are going out," Jake said. "Don't you think she knows already?"

"And Sally would try to put a stop to it," added Melody. "She made a great speech at practice yesterday about school spirit."

"It was amazing," said Emily. "Sally's amazing."

Alexis hoped her friends were right. Maybe Sally could make a difference. And maybe her article would help, too.

MAIN STREET 4:55 P.M.

As Sally Johnson Rollerbladed away from her house, she was listening to her Walkman and thinking about the Cougars. She was headed for the beach where some kids she knew from Claymore High's football team and cheer squad liked to hang out. They'd been Bulldog athletes and played in the Bulldog-Cougar games in middle school. Sally wanted to talk to those guys about what the Cougars had done at CMS. She'd remind them that the Cougars played dirty and how their cheerleaders treated the Bulldog cheerleaders at the game the year before.

Sally was so distracted by her thoughts that she didn't notice Joan coming from the other direction.

But Joan saw Sally. She admired how beautiful Sally looked rolling along the sidewalk, her long blond hair flying out behind her. I'd love to Rollerblade, she thought. But I can't. Not as long as I live with Michelle Russo and Paul Chazen. Rollerblading was just one more thing that they considered frivolous and dangerous.

Joan figured that Sally would roll right by her. But when Sally finally saw Joan, she did a little turn and stopped. As she punched off her cassette player and pulled off her headphones, she said, "Hi, Joanie. What's up?"

"Not much," Joan answered. As soon as the words were out of her mouth, Joan knew they sounded dumb. She thought, If I don't say something interesting, Sally will be sorry she even stopped. Maybe I should tell her about the meeting we just had. She'll want to stop any trouble with Santa Rosa, too.

But before Joan could say anything, Sally picked up the conversation herself. "Joanie, you're doing great at the stunts for the center cheer. I had a captains' meeting with Coach this afternoon. She's thinks you're great, too."

"Thanks," Joan said.

"And," Sally continued, "Sam Paetro is going to run a clinic for the squad."

"Sam Paetro?" Joan said. "The man who works for CHEER USA?"

"Yup," Sally said. "He'll work with us on tumbling and stunts after school on Thursdays."

Joan's heart sank. She had her piano lesson on Thursday afternoons now.

"Isn't that awesome?" Sally said. "We start next week."

"Great," Joan said, forcing a smile.

As Sally bladed off, Joan thought, How can I take those tumbling classes? I can't ask Mr. Richter to change my class again without telling my parents. I have to make up something that I have to do after school that they'll think is really important. I'll have to lie to my parents again. I hate lying, but I love cheerleading. Why do I have to do something I hate in order to do something I love? It isn't fair.

She turned the corner onto Delhaven Drive and walked slowly toward her house.

Sally was already three blocks away from Joan and skating down Main Street. She loved to Rollerblade on the busy street of shops where plenty of people would see her. Things were going great! Darryl was worked up about the Cougars, and she was going to talk to the high school guys.

Now, what can I do to get revenge on those Cougar cheerleaders for what they did to us last year? Sally wondered. Whatever it was, it had to be something no one would guess she had planned. It should be something that would hit the Cougar cheerleaders just before they went out to cheer. Something to shake them up.

She'd teach those cheerleaders that they couldn't push her squad around.

CLAYMORE BEACH 5:30 P.M.

After the meeting at the Bulldog Café, Adam and Melody walked home together.

"You want to walk on the beach partway?" Adam asked.

"Sure," Melody agreed. "Maybe we'll see a dolphin."

"Have you ever tried to keep up with them by running along the beach?" Adam asked.

"I was just thinking about how I used to love to do that," Melody told him.

When they got to the beach they took off their shoes so they could walk in the surf. "I've been meaning to tell you," Adam said. "You were really great cheering at the pep rally."

"Thanks," said Melody. "I'd never been to a pep rally before. It was fun. I just hope the game will be as much fun. I'm so afraid there will be an ugly scene with bad vibes."

"Are you going to try to talk Darryl out of whatever he's got planned?"

"If he mentions it again," she said. "But I figure Sally will take care of that."

They walked along without talking for a while. Finally Adam said, "Has Darryl asked you out or anything?"

"You're kidding, right?" said Melody.

"Just wondered," Adam said. "I mean, if he's been friendly and everything, I thought maybe . . ."

"Come on, Adam," Melody protested. "Darryl is this big deal captain-of-the-football-team, boyfriend-of-a-captain-of-the-cheer-squad ninth-grader. I'm a lowly seventh-grader."

"You seem older than a seventh-grader," Adam said.

Melody remembered that Darryl had said the same thing. But she didn't tell Adam. It seemed like a good time to change the subject. "Joan is an amazing flyer," she said. "Everyone's talking about it."

"Never say anything like that in front of our parents," Adam said.

"How come?" asked Melody.

"They don't know that cheering involves gymnastics," he said, "which they consider dangerous and a waste of time."

"That must be tough on Joan," Melody said. "She's such a great athlete. There must be lots of sports she'd love to do."

"It is tough on her," Adam said. "I think sometimes our parents are stricter with her than they are with me. Most of it is because she's younger. But still, sometimes it seems unfair. She has to be home an hour before I do on school nights. All because her piano teacher said she wasn't improving fast enough."

"Is that why she's having an extra lesson to-day?" Melody asked.

Adam stopped himself from telling Melody that Joan didn't have a piano lesson at five o'clock. He didn't want Joan's friends to know that she lied to them. But she had. And she'd been lying a lot to their parents lately. He saw trouble ahead for his sister. And he didn't know how to stop it.

Melody spotted Sally hanging out on a blanket with a couple of older guys and a girl. They were talking and laughing. Sally fits right in with those older kids, thought Melody.

"Look!" Adam said, pointing to the water. "A dolphin. Follow my finger. Keep looking."

In a few seconds Melody saw a gray comma-shaped dolphin break through the surface of the water, arch through the air, and knife back into the water.

"Come on!" Melody shouted. "Let's try to keep up with it."

She and Adam laughed as they ran along the beach together. The sea air filled Melody's lungs, and the wind whipped around her body. One of the things she had loved most about living in Miami was living near the ocean. She loved the sea and the life in it — especially dolphins.

She wasn't living in Miami, but she still lived near the water. And she had a new friend who seemed to love it as much as she did.

DELHAVEN DRIVE 9:05 P.M.

Joan had tried to do her homework. She couldn't. Not when all she could think about was her parents and Sam Paetro's tumbling clinic. If I spend all this time worrying, she thought, I won't do my homework. Then I'll get bad grades, and I'll be in really big trouble. There's nothing more important to my parents than school grades.

There was a tap on her door.

"What?" she yelled.

"It's me," Adam answered. "Can I come in?"

"Sure," she said.

He came in, closed the door behind him, and sat on the edge of her bed.

Joan was feeling irritated with her brother. He hasn't done anything particularly wrong, she thought, except maybe slip into my new group of friends.

"What do you want, Adam?" she asked without looking up from her notebook.

"Nothing special," he answered. "Just wondered what you were doing."

"What does it look like I'm doing?" she snapped. "What do we ever do around here at night? Certainly not watch television like normal people."

"Joanie . . ."

She swiveled around and glared at him. How many times did she have to tell him to call her Joan, not Joanie?

"Joan," he said, correcting himself. "I just think . . . I mean, you seem so angry about this cheering stuff and mother and father."

"Sh-sh," she hissed. "They'll hear you."

"No, they won't," he said. "They're in the living room reading and listening to opera."

Joan knew that she was being mean to Adam. She wasn't being fair. After all, Adam was her brother and her friend. Maybe he could help her. She looked up at him and closed her notebook. "I hate the way they don't approve of anything I want to do," she told him.

"Maybe now that you're older they won't mind about the gymnastics," he suggested. "It's not like it's really dangerous. You should try talking to them about it again. I'd help you."

"Talk to them!" Joan exclaimed. "Are you kidding? Or are you completely out of your mind?"

"I just thought . . ." he said.

"Think a little harder," she said. "I'm the one who had to quit gymnastics. I'm the one who has to be home at five. I can't even stay out with my friends. Pretty soon I'll be home all the time, and I won't have any friends."

"Your friends understand," Adam said. "They feel sorry for you."

"What?" Joan shouted as she jumped up from the chair and ran over to him. She glared at Adam.

Adam realized his mistake. His sister had lied to her friends because she didn't want them to know that she had strict parents. And he had told Melody.

"Who did you tell?" she asked angrily. "What did you say?"

"Nothing," answered Adam. "I — "

Joan gripped his arm. "Adam Russo-Chazen," she said. "If you don't tell me what you said I'll tell everyone every little stupid thing I know about you — like that you sucked your thumb until you were *eight years old.*"

"I just talked to Melody," he said. "On the way home. She was saying what a great flyer you are and I said that it was too bad that our parents are so against cheering. I don't think you should be lying to your friends, Joan. I think — "

"I don't care what you think," she said, interrupting him. "You are such a creep. You're as bad as Mother and Father." Tears sprang to her eyes.

She turned away from him. She wasn't going to let Adam see her cry. That would just prove that she was a baby.

"Get out of my room," she shouted. "Get out NOW!"

She heard Adam stand up and walk to the door. "I'm sorry, Joan," he said. "I didn't mean to — "

"You just want Melody to think you're a big shot," she said, "so 'psychological' and kind."

But Adam was gone. He hadn't even heard her. Joan locked the door to her room and threw herself on her bed.

Everybody would know. They'd know that her parents wouldn't let her do *anything* that was fun. They'd think that *she* wasn't any fun. And they'd all be talking about her like she was some pitiful little thing.

I am pitiful, Joan thought as she rolled over and buried her wet face in the pillow.

CMS SMALL GYM. WEDNESDAY 3:30 P.M.

The cheerleaders sat in two rows, their legs stretched out in front of them.

"Reach to the ceiling," Coach instructed. "One. Two. Three. Four. Now drop and reach for those toes. Keep your legs straight."

Emily glanced at her watch as she bent over. Ten more minutes of stretches.

She looked under her right arm. Melody was lying flat out over her legs.

She looked under her left arm. Joan, the human pretzel, had opened her legs in a perfect split and was lying flat on the floor between them. Sally could do that, too. And Mae. But not me, thought Emily. I'll never even come close to doing that. I can't even reach my toes or stretch out my back in this position, because my huge stomach is in the way.

Coach had announced that next week they were starting a clinic with a CHEER USA coach. "Sam Paetro will move your tumbling to a new level," Coach promised.

Everybody's tumbling but mine, thought Emily. I can't even do a handspring. And my jumps aren't as high as the other cheerleaders'. I know they aren't. The only thing I'm good at is yelling the chants and cheers. Big deal.

After warm-ups Sally led them in jumps. Then they tumbled. Finally, Coach called a five-minute break. "There's a cooler by the door," she said. "Hydrate, girls."

Maria, another seventh-grade cheerleader, walked with Emily toward the cooler. "Did you hear what's going on?" Maria whispered in Emily's ear. "About the Bulldogs and the Cougars?"

Emily decided to play dumb. Maybe that way she could learn more. "What?" she asked.

"Some people in town and a couple of guys from the team. They're going to get back at the Cougars — on Friday night," Maria said. "Isn't that great?"

Emily wanted to tell Maria that she didn't think it was great at all. Then, of course, Maria would think she was a wimp or a goody-goody. But if I don't say what I really believe, Emily decided, how can I expect to stop it? By the time she figured all that out, they'd reached the cooler and the rest of the cheerleaders.

"Don't tell anyone," Maria whispered, and she was lost in the crowd of girls reaching for drinks.

Emily picked out an apple juice. She turned it over and read the label. One hundred fifty calories. Even things that were good for you had calories. She put the juice back and took a bottle of water. Zero calories. She noticed that Sally was drinking water, too.

Sally felt someone's eyes on her. She turned and saw Emily. Sally remembered that she wanted to talk to Emily and motioned her to meet in a corner away from the other girls.

I bet she wants to talk to me about the Bulldog-Cougar stuff, Emily thought. I'll tell her about our meeting about what to do to calm things down. And without naming names I'll tell her that some of the cheerleaders don't have the right spirit. That they aren't following what Sally said at the Monday practice.

Emily was about to say all that when she met Sally at the corner of the gym. But Sally spoke first. "I wondered how your diet is going."

Emily was surprised by the question. Sally must think she was really fat.

"Okay, I guess," Emily said. "I'm not eating as much."

"Good for you," Sally said.

Emily wanted to tell Sally how hard it was to diet. How she got so hungry that she stuffed herself and then felt awful after.

"You need to work on your jumps more, Emily," Sally told her. "You need cleaner jumps if we're going to place at CHEER USA."

"Okay," said Emily. She smiled so Sally would know that she was grateful for the help. But she wanted to cry. It was all too difficult.

Sally beamed Emily a big smile. "You can do it, Emily," she said. "I know you can. Get your sister to help you. She's a fabulous cheerleader."

Emily stopped herself from telling Sally that Lynn had worked with her on cheering all summer. Because then Sally would know the truth about her.

She was never going to be a better cheer-leader.

CMS COURTYARD 5:00 P.M.

Melody Max sat on a bench in the courtyard and did her math homework. Her mother would be by any minute to pick her up for a big grocery shop.

"Hey," a voice boomed in her ear.

Melody was so startled she jumped and let out a little yelp.

"Sorry," Darryl said. "Didn't mean to scare you."

"It's okay," Melody said. "You just finish practice?"

"Yeah. And we're looking good. We'll whip those Cougars."

Melody felt relieved. Darryl understood that the way to get back at the Cougars was to win the game. "So the pranks are off?" she said.

Darryl laughed. "No way. When the Cougars roll into Claymore they'll already know who is going to win that game."

"What are you going to do?" Melody asked, trying to hide her alarm.

"You'll see," he said. "Everyone will."

"Tell me," she said in a hushed voice.

Darryl shook his head. "It's all a major secret," he said.

"I just wonder what you could do after what they did to us."

Darryl looked around the courtyard. There were still a few kids there, but none of them was within hearing distance. "We're sneaking into Santa Rosa the night before the game," he began.

"Who?" she asked.

"A few of us guys from CMS and some of the high school guys, you know, who used to play CMS football," Darryl answered. "We're going to spray-paint their buses — all of them — with BULLDOGS WILL WIN. Everyone will see it. Kids getting on those buses. People in town. This cool quarterback from Claymore High has this paint that doesn't come off and is, like, impossible to cover up. They'll have to drive those buses here. They bring loads of kids to the game. But that's not all."

"Not all?" Melody said.

"You're going to love this," Darryl began in his slow drawl. "There's this stuff we're going to put under the hoods that will smoke up when they start the buses. It's stinky smoke. Man, you wouldn't want to be on one of those buses when that happens."

Melody noticed her mother driving up to the school. She didn't have time to try to convince Darryl *not* to do all the things he was so excited about.

"Does Sally know about all this?" she asked as she picked up her books.

He nodded.

Melody's mother honked the horn to let Melody know she was there . . . and waiting.

"I have to go," Melody told Darryl.

"Don't tell anybody about the plan," he said. "We want it to be a surprise. I just wanted you to know that we're taking care of things. You don't have to worry."

I'm plenty worried, Melody thought as she went toward the car. She imagined school buses — loaded with kids — filling up with smelly smoke. Smoke that could hurt someone. At least Sally knows, Melody thought as she got in the car.

32 MAIN STREET. 5:15 P.M.

Jake was dribbling a basketball in front of his garage. He stopped, turned, and made a hook shot from under the basket.

As he grabbed the ball, Jake saw Alexis biking across the hotel parking lot and waved.

Alexis waved back. Suddenly she felt a little funny. She'd been to Jake's dozens of times — but never without Emily.

Alexis rode her bike into the Feders' backyard and pulled up to Jake.

"Want to shoot some hoops before we work on the article?" he asked.

69

"Sure," she said.

They played a little one-on-one.

"You're good," Jake told her after Alexis sunk her third basket.

It was so much fun. Alexis couldn't stop smiling the whole time. She remembered how she hated smiling for cheerleading. But basketball was different.

Basketball was the sport she loved, especially when she was shooting baskets with Jake.

THE MANOR HOTEL. 5:35 P.M.

Emily was at her desk doing her math homework. She looked at the first problem and wrote down some numbers. But all she could think about was food. She was so hungry. And she was mad at herself for going off her diet last night. Well, today she hadn't eaten anything, and she wouldn't later, either. The weird thing was that the only person who knew she was on a diet was Sally. Emily wondered if it would help if she told someone besides Sally that she was trying desperately to lose weight. Someone she could *really* talk to. Someone like Alexis. Alexis was her best friend. Yes, she'd talk to Alexis about it.

Emily picked up her phone and speed-dialed Alexis's father's apartment.

The answering machine picked up after four

rings. "Hi, Alexis," Emily told the machine after the message and beep, "it's me. Call, okay?"

Emily tried to go back to her math homework. It was no use. She couldn't concentrate. Should she tell Jake about the diet? Jake was so sweet he'd just tell her that she wasn't fat and didn't need to lose weight. But being around Jake might make her feel better. She closed her math book. She'd go over to his house and hang out until dinner. She could do her homework later.

When she stood up she felt a little dizzy from not eating. She held onto the desk until her balance came back. Then she went to the window to see if Jake was outside. She saw him dribbling a basketball. Then she saw that Alexis was with him. Alexis! That's where she is, thought Emily as she headed for her door. He must be helping her with her article. She can come over here when they finish, and I'll tell her about the diet.

By the time Emily ran over to Jake's house, Alexis and Jake weren't outside anymore. Emily went to the kitchen door and looked through the screen. They were sitting at the kitchen table having a cold drink and talking about Alexis's article. Their backs were to her so they didn't see her. They were busy working. Emily turned and walked home.

Alexis and Jake had more important things to do than talk to a fat, famished cheerleader.

SQUEEZE. THURSDAY 8:00 A.M.

Melody waited in front of the juice bar. Even though Darryl had asked her not to tell anyone about the plan to strike back at the Cougars, she felt that she had to tell her friends. They couldn't expect Sally to stop the vandalism all on her own. So Melody had called everyone and asked them to meet her at the juice bar before school. She had some more information on the Cougar-Bulldog case.

Melody saw Jake and Emily heading toward her from one direction and Alexis from another. Before they reached her, a car pulled up, and Joan and Adam jumped out.

"Good-bye, Mother," Melody heard Adam say. Joan's mother said something to Adam and Joan in another language. Melody thought it was French.

"I will," Joan told her mother. "I'll be there."

Melody's parents had always given her a lot of freedom. She wondered what it would be like to have parents who were strict.

"Was your mother speaking French to you?" Melody asked Joan and Adam.

"*Oui,*" answered Adam with a grin.

Joan wasn't smiling. She seemed tense and

72

grumpy. Melody wanted to say something, but she wasn't sure what would make Joan feel better. She just smiled at Joan and walked with her to meet the others.

The six friends went across the street to the park and sat on the grass. Melody told them what Darryl and his friends had planned for the Cougars.

"We have to stop them," Emily said.

"They have everything organized, right down to what kind of paint they're using," Jake pointed out. "Our articles aren't going to change their minds."

"What else can we do?" Alexis asked.

"We should try to talk to Darryl," Adam suggested. "Get him to change his mind."

"He could get in big trouble over this," Melody said. "Like be suspended or even kicked off the team. I wonder if he's thought about that."

"Don't you think Sally will keep Darryl from going ahead with the prank?" Joan asked.

"I'm sure she's tried," Melody said. "But I think she needs help. I mean, Darryl said she knows, but he's still bragging about what he's going to do to get back at the Cougars."

"You should talk to Darryl, Melody," Jake said. "Tell him how serious this is."

"And that it's dangerous for innocent people,

like the kids on those buses," added Emily.

"Tell him the story you told us about the tear gas at that fraternity house," suggested Joan.

"Darryl's a nice guy," Alexis said. "He probably just hasn't thought about all of this."

"Okay," Melody said. "I'll try."

"Maybe you and Sally could talk to him together," said Adam. "You know, join forces."

"Good idea," agreed Emily.

Melody hesitated. Even though Sally was always nice to her, sometimes she didn't think Sally really liked her. It wasn't anything Sally did or that she could put a finger on. Just a feeling. A weird feeling.

"Maybe it's better if Sally and I approach Darryl separately," Melody suggested. "The message could be more powerful that way."

They all agreed. Melody only hoped that she could pull this off.

It was a big responsibility.

CMS COURTYARD 8:25 A.M.

Melody walked with Joan and Emily across the courtyard.

"There he is," Joan whispered to Melody. "Talking to Sally."

Melody saw Sally and Darryl standing under one of the courtyard palm trees. Sally was tilted back against the tree trunk. Darryl put one hand on the tree and leaned forward to whisper something in her ear. Sally laughed, gave Darryl a quick kiss on the cheek, and ran over to a group of her friends.

"Here's your chance, Melody," Joan said. "He's all alone."

Emily gave Melody a little push in Darryl's direction. "Go. Do it," she instructed. "Good luck."

As Melody walked toward Darryl she wondered if she'd be able to stop his plan. She looked at her watch. It was almost time for homeroom. She didn't have much time. She started toward him.

Two of Darryl's friends from the football team ran over to him. Darryl said something to them, and one of the guys hit Darryl on the back as if to congratulate him. Melody was sure they were talking about all the stuff they were going to do in Santa Rosa on Friday night.

She turned back to her friends and shrugged her shoulders. She'd lost her chance. She'd have to find another time when she could talk to Darryl Budd alone.

Emily and Joan came up on either side of her.

"Joan has an idea," Emily said.

"You should write Darryl a note," Joan suggested. "Tell him you have something important to discuss with him. Ask him to meet you someplace — I don't know where — you pick it out."

"But it shouldn't be at school," Emily added. "He's so popular you'll be interrupted."

"He'll think I'm asking him on a date," Melody said. "And I'm not. It's too embarrassing."

"*You* know you're not asking him out," Emily said, "and he'll know it when you meet him."

"*If* he'll meet me," said Melody. "What if he ignores my note but tells everyone I asked him out?"

"This is important, Melody," said Joan. "It's the only way."

The morning bell rang and a bunch of kids swarmed around them as they walked into school. They couldn't talk privately anymore.

"Okay," Melody told her friends. "It's worth a try."

When she reached homeroom she opened her notebook and wrote:

Darryl. I need to talk to you. It's urgent. Could you meet me on the beach in front of Joe's Seafood Shack around 4:00? No need to answer this note unless you can't make it. I hope you can. Melody

Melody folded the paper in half and put it in her pocket. She'd have to slip it to Darryl later. Privately.

Between first and second periods Melody

took a detour through the ninth-grade corridor on her way to math class. She saw Darryl coming down the hall with a bunch of other guys. He noticed her and smiled but kept walking. No way can I give it to him when he's in a crowd like that, she thought. She kept an eye on Darryl until she saw what room he went in. Then she went back to the first floor. Oh, boy, she thought, it is so obvious that I was waiting for him. He really will think I'm chasing after him.

She felt her face flush with embarrassment, and she hadn't even given him the note yet.

Between the next two periods Melody went back to the ninth-grade corridor and headed straight for the room she'd seen Darryl go into at the beginning of the second period. When he came out she was ready. She quickly thrust the note in his hand, whispered, "Private," and disappeared into the crowd of ninth-graders.

CLAYMORE BEACH 4:15 P.M.

Melody sat on the sand facing the ocean. She reviewed in her mind all the things she wanted to tell Darryl. She looked at her watch. Four-sixteen. What if he didn't show up? She'd wait until four-thirty. The next time she looked down the beach she saw Darryl running across the sand toward her.

"Hey," he said. He was breathless from running. The late afternoon sunlight made a halo around his blond hair. He plopped down in the sand beside her. A huge smile spread across his face. "I figured out why you want to see me."

"You did?" Melody said. Please, she prayed, please don't think I want to go out with you. It would be too embarrassing.

He leaned toward her and said, "You want in on it."

"In on it?" she asked with surprise.

"In on the prank we're playing in Santa Rosa," he said. "But we're not bringing girls."

Melody gave a little laugh. "That's not why I wanted to talk to you," she said. "It's something else. Something very important. But I need you to just listen. So don't interrupt me. Okay?"

"Okay," he agreed.

"When I finish what I have to say you can argue with me," she continued. "I like to argue. I think arguing is very cool." Melody watched Darryl's blank expression. She knew that she was babbling.

Darryl ran his hands through his hair. "Melody, what are you getting at?" he said. "I've got stuff to take care of, you know. So hit a point, will you?"

No more stalling, thought Melody. Time to be blunt.

"Darryl, I don't think you should vandalize

the Cougar school buses. You have to stop it from happening."

Darryl put up a hand. "Whoa. This is why you wanted to meet me?"

Melody pushed his hand down with hers. "Darryl, you promised to hear me out. Listen. I want to explain why."

Melody explained her reasons for not vandalizing the buses. Darryl fidgeted and threatened to leave once, but in the end he let her finish what she'd planned to say.

"Okay," she finally said. "Your turn to talk."

At that moment a volleyball hit Darryl on the head.

"Hey, goofball," someone shouted. "Can't you leave the girls alone for five minutes?"

Darryl and Melody looked up. Three guys in bathing suits were running toward them.

Darryl threw the ball back, then turned to Melody and hissed, "Don't say a word about this. Not a word."

"Just think about what I said," Melody told him.

The ball came back. This time it was headed straight for Melody. She reached up, caught it, and tossed it back — not too far since the guys had almost reached them.

Darryl jumped to his feet. "Let's go," he told his friends. "Do we have enough for a game?"

"Yeah. But there's room for your little friend," said a red-haired guy Melody recognized from the football team. He winked at Melody. "If she wants to play."

Before Melody could answer, Darryl said, "She has to go."

As Melody walked off the beach she saw a bunch of guys and girls organizing into two teams on either side of a volleyball net. One of them was Sally.

Sally saw Melody, too. Did Darryl ask Melody to go for a walk on the beach? she wondered. Or was it the other way around? She intended to find out.

Darryl tossed Sally the ball and headed toward her.

"Didn't know you had a hot after-school date," she said in a teasing voice.

Darryl's face flushed. "We were just talking," he said. "She's a seventh-grader."

"I know," said Sally. "I thought maybe you were baby-sitting."

Randy, a halfback on the Bulldog team, overheard Sally and Darryl. "You jealous, Sally?" he asked, teasing.

"Are you kidding?" Sally answered. She smiled, but she was furious. Not at Darryl. But at Randy for thinking she'd be jealous. No way was she going have a reputation for being jealous.

Not over Darryl Budd. Not when she could be dating high school guys. The only reason she was bothering with this ninth-grade crowd was because she wanted to be the most popular, most everything at CMS.

"Randy," she cooed as she threw him her biggest, flirtiest smile, "let's play."

When the game was in motion Sally kept her eye on the ball and did her part to win for her side. But her mind was elsewhere. What had Melody and Darryl talked about? Was the sophisticated seventh-grader from Miami after her boyfriend? Well, she couldn't have him.

Not during football season.

BULLDOG CAFÉ 5:00 P.M.

Adam, Emily, Jake, and Alexis were waiting for Melody. Adam hoped that Melody didn't have a crush on Darryl. He didn't want her to be hurt. After all, Darryl did have a girlfriend. He wished Melody would hurry up. She was very late.

"It's too bad Joan couldn't come," Alexis said.

"How come she couldn't?" asked Jake.

"Piano lesson," Adam said. "Joan's really good."

Adam took a gulp of his lemonade. That was okay to say, he thought. I didn't make Joan look bad, and I didn't lie. Not this time.

Adam looked around the table. Alexis and Jake were talking about the newspapers that were coming out the next day. Emily was half listening to them while she built a little house out of a brownie and broken pieces of chocolate chip cookies. Adam sighed and reached for another cookie. As he took a bite he noticed Melody walking toward the café. "Here she is," he told the others.

"I can't wait to hear what happened," Emily said.

The expression on Melody's face as she came closer already told Adam that her meeting with Darryl hadn't gone well.

"What happened?" Alexis asked as she poured Melody a glass of lemonade. Adam pushed the plate of cookies and brownies in Melody's direction.

"Well," Melody said as she sat down, "I told Darryl what I had to say. But his friends came by as soon as I finished my list of reasons. Darryl was not happy about what I had to say, I can tell you that. He wanted me out of there."

"You told him about maybe getting suspended and thrown off the football team?" Emily asked.

Melody nodded. "I told him everything."

"Maybe he'll think about what you said," added Alexis.

"I hope you're right," Melody said. She looked around the table. "So what has been happening here?"

"The *Bulldog Edition* is being printed now," Jake said. He looked at his watch. "I'm picking it up in an hour. Don't forget to wear your uniforms to school tomorrow. And be at school fifteen minutes early to hand the papers out."

"I'll remind Joan," Adam said.

"My mother is running Alexis's article and Jake's editorial on the sports page of the Claymore and the Santa Rosa editions of the paper tomorrow," said Melody.

"Great," said Adam.

"So if the prank does happen," said Alexis, "both towns will know that most Bulldogs weren't behind it."

"What else can we do?" asked Jake.

The five friends looked at one another and thought for a minute.

"I can't think of anything else," said Emily.

"Me, either," said Jake.

Adam looked at his watch. "I have to go," he said.

"I'll go with you," said Melody as she stood up. She smiled at Emily. "Thanks for the great snack. The house you made with the brownie and cookies is cute. You going to eat it now?"

Emily shook her head. "I made it for Lily," she said.

DOLPHIN COURT APARTMENTS 9:00 P.M.

Melody checked her e-mail. No messages from her friends. But there was one from her dad.

> Hey there, Maxi. What'd you think of my new on-air jacket? And check out the tie tomorrow. Let me know if it's too loud. Or too quiet. Or too anything not cool enough for your fancy taste. I miss having you here to help pick out my ties. Miss you period. Good luck with that big game on Saturday. Love. Dad.

The only time Melody could see her father was when he did the weather forecast from Miami at 8:15 each weekday morning. She'd missed him that morning because of the meeting at Squeeze. And she'd have to leave the house early the next day, too. She'd better write to him.

> Missed your spot this A.M. and will tomorrow, too. Have (and had) to be at school early. Lots going on in prep for big game on Saturday. More about that later. But puh-lease

wear that jacket and tie next week. Promise I
will check them out. Your Max.

She pointed the cursor at "reply to sender"
and clicked the mouse.

Now I'll write to Tina, Melody thought. I'll tell
her what's been going down with this Cougar-
Bulldog game. She started the letter and stopped
to reread what she'd written. All that was going
on in Claymore the last few days was just too
complicated to put into words. She deleted everything she wrote. Maybe when it's all over I'll be
able to write about it, Melody thought. Then the
story will have an ending.

But how will it end? she wondered.

CMS COURTYARD. FRIDAY 8:15 A.M.

Joan and Emily held a pile of *Bulldog Edition* copies and stood near the entrance to the
courtyard with four other cheerleaders. With
each paper Joan handed out she said, "Check
out the sports column and the editorial page."

As Alexis walked across the courtyard she
saw kids reading the *Bulldog Edition* and knew
that a lot of them were reading her column.
Would people agree with what she wrote? Would
her article make a difference?

Melody walked around the courtyard making

sure everyone had a paper. She spotted Darryl with two of his football friends. She went over to them and asked, "Everybody here get a paper?"

"Yeah, we got it," said a cute short guy. He patted a folded copy of the *Bulldog Edition* sticking out of his back pocket.

"Well, check out the sports column and the editorial page," Melody said. "It's all about the rivalry with the Cougars and the game tomorrow."

"*We're* the game tomorrow," said a big guy the kids called The Truck.

"You sure are," Melody said.

Darryl didn't say anything, but he was staring at Melody. She looked him right in the eye and said, "We're behind you one hundred percent."

Darryl half smiled as he told her, "We'll give you a good game. The Cougars are going to know who's in charge." He winked at her, turned, and walked away. His friends went with him.

Sally stood across the courtyard watching Melody with Darryl. She needed to know what Melody knew about tonight. Was Darryl talking to her about it right now?

"Melody," she called. "Over here."

Melody looked up and saw Sally motioning for her to come over. As she walked toward Sally she hoped that Sally had an idea to stop Darryl.

"Hey," Sally said as Melody reached her. "Saw

you talking to Darryl. He's pretty worked up over the game, isn't he?"

"That's for sure," Melody said.

"Well, you can see why he would be," Sally said. "It's an important game. Especially after what the Cougars did."

"I just hope kids from Claymore don't play pranks in Santa Rosa tonight," Melody said.

"You don't need to worry about that," Sally told her.

"Did Darryl say they called it off?" asked Melody.

"Called what off?" asked Sally. She'd play dumb with Melody until she found out how much she knew.

"The prank he was planning," Melody answered. "You know, on the Santa Rosa school buses. He told me you knew. I've been trying to convince him to drop it, too."

So Darryl has been blabbing to Melody about the plans to vandalize the Santa Rosa buses, thought Sally. If he told her, he's probably told a lot of other people. And everyone he's told has told others. And that was not cool.

"Don't worry about it, Melody," she said. "I'm sure if you spoke to him he'll do the right thing."

"I hope so," Melody said. "I'm afraid that people could get hurt. And that Darryl would be kicked off the team."

The bell rang for homeroom.

"Don't worry about anything," Sally told her. "Just go out there tomorrow and cheer for CMS."

"I will," Melody promised.

After Melody left, Sally quickly scanned the crowd for Darryl. She finally found him heading toward the school entrance and ran over to him.

"Hey, babe," Darryl said when he saw her.

Sally threw an arm around his neck. "What's up, Darryl? You keeping yourself out of trouble?"

"I'm trying to," Darryl answered. He looked around to be sure no one could overhear them. "Listen, Sally," he said in a low voice, "this whole thing with Santa Rosa. What if I get caught? I could get kicked out of school."

Sally thought, Sure. Now that you've blabbered it all over town. She didn't want a boyfriend who was a loser. Being kicked off the football team, maybe even out of school, was definitely not cool. And not part of her plan.

"Word has gotten out that something is up," she said. "It's possible you could get in trouble. Maybe you should back out."

"Yeah, that's what I've been thinking, too," Darryl told her. "But Dave Grafton and Ray Torres have it all planned."

"You can tell them that a lot of people seem to know about it. Tell them it would be bad for them if they went through with the plan." She gave him her special smile. "I don't want anything bad to happen to you."

"Thanks, babe," he said. "You're the best."

"You, too," she said.

Even though Darryl's backing out, Sally thought, I can still take care of the Cougar cheerleaders tomorrow — and I don't need anyone's help to do it. A genuine smile spread over her face as she walked toward the front door of the school with Darryl.

Joan bent to pick up a pile of extra newspapers from the steps. As she stood she saw Sally and Darryl going into the school arm in arm. That is so sweet, she thought. The captain of the football team and the co-captain of the cheer squad.

The perfect couple giving their all to CMS.

CMS SMALL GYM 4:15 P.M.

It was the last cheerleading practice before the big game. After the warm-up and some jumping and tumbling practice the girls took a short break. Emily felt tired and hungry. I had a good diet day, she told herself. Maybe tomorrow my uniform won't be so tight.

"Time to draw names," Coach announced. She held up a baseball cap. "Mae, explain it to the new girls."

"The football players' names are in the hat," she said. "We each pick a name. If your player gets a touchdown or does something awesome in the game, you'll do the individual cheer for him."

"So gather round," Coach said. "The co-captains will draw names, then we'll go by class, starting with the ninth-graders."

"I want Randy," Maria whispered to Emily as they joined the circle surrounding Coach. "Randy's so cute, and he always makes a touchdown. Who do you want?"

"I don't know," Emily answered.

Melody and Joan moved over to be near Emily.

"I hope Sally gets Darryl," Joan said.

"Me, too," Emily agreed. "It would be so romantic."

Sally opened her slip and rolled her eyes.

"Guess she didn't get him," said Joan.

"The problem is, some guys, like the linemen, never get cheered for," explained Emily. "Nobody wants to draw their names."

"It looks like Sally picked one," Joan said. "I wonder who will pick Darryl."

Next the ninth-graders drew. Then the eighth-graders.

"Who picked Darryl?" C.J. asked as the seventh-graders lined up for their turn.

None of the ninth- or eighth-graders answered.

"It looks like a seventh-grader will be cheering for him," Mae said.

"I hope it's me!" Maria loudly exclaimed.

Everybody laughed, but the noise quieted down while the seventh-graders picked.

Emily drew first. She almost hoped she wouldn't get Darryl. If she did she'd have to do a jump all by herself. Everyone would see how bad she was. She opened the slip and read it out loud. "Willy Stanton," she said.

"He's a linesman," Maria told her.

Melody went next.

Sally watched her carefully.

Melody opened the slip, smiled, and held it up. "Darryl," she said.

Everyone clapped.

I hate that girl, Sally thought as she joined in the applause, I totally hate her.

As soon as the other seventh-graders had drawn names, Coach called out, "Let's go. Line up for the sideline cheer. Let's see toe jumps on the C and M and make them nice and high and point those toes. Then hit the visual formation on the S."

The cheerleaders lined up side by side and shouted, **"HEY, FANS! LET'S CHEER. GO, CMS!"**

Emily jumped on the C and went right back up again for the M. She remembered being in the air and landing. But the next thing she knew, she was lying on the floor and couldn't remember falling. Everything looked blurry. Slowly, Melody's face and Joan's face came into focus.

"Are you all right?" Melody asked.

"What happened?" asked Joan.

As more girls gathered around Emily, Coach pushed past them, told them to back up, and knelt down next to Emily.

Emily propped herself up on her elbows. "When I came down from the second jump everything was kind of spinning," she said as tears sprang to her eyes.

She tried to stand up, but Coach put her hand out to stop her. "Stay there for a minute," she said as she put her fingers around Emily's wrist to take her pulse and asked, "Do you still feel dizzy?"

"Just a little," Emily said softly.

"Are you nauseous?"

Emily shook her head no.

"Did you hit your head when you fell?"

"I don't think so," Emily answered. She felt her head. "It doesn't hurt or anything."

"Pain anywhere else?"

"Uh-uh," Emily answered, shaking her head.

Emily looked around at the faces of the other cheerleaders leaning over to see her. They all looked worried.

"I'm okay," Emily told them. "I'm not dizzy at all anymore."

Coach looked up at the girls, too. "Mae, get me a bottle of water and an orange juice," she ordered. "The rest of you can leave now. Be here an hour before the game tomorrow, that's 12:30. I'm going to take Emily home."

Melody touched Emily on the shoulder and said, "I'll call you later."

"Me, too," added Joan.

"Thanks," Emily told her

Mae brought over the drinks. As Emily drank the water, Coach said, "What have you eaten today, Emily, starting with breakfast?"

"A piece of toast," Emily told her.

"Not enough," Coach said. "And for lunch?"

"An apple."

"Not enough," Coach repeated. She handed Emily the orange juice to drink.

After Emily drank some of the juice she stood up. She felt fine. "I'm okay now," she told Coach. "You don't have to take me home."

"Yes, I do," Coach insisted. "We need to talk."

Emily felt a wave of fear go through her. What was Coach going to say?

COACH CORTES'S CAR 4:45 P.M.

As Coach drove her car out of the school parking lot, she turned to face Emily and asked, "Are you on a diet?"

"Sort of," Emily said.

"You don't need to be," Coach told her. "You're a fine size."

"Everyone else on the squad is smaller than me," Emily said.

"So what?" Coach said. "People come in all sizes. You are not fat, Emily Granger. And not eating enough can affect your cheering. Food gives you energy. You need your energy to be a good cheerleader."

She doesn't think I cheer good enough either, Emily thought.

"Besides," Coach continued, "it's normal for a girl your age to put on a little weight."

She does think I'm overweight, Emily thought. She's just worried about my feelings. She's being extra nice to me because I'm a Granger.

Coach stopped the car in front of the hotel and turned to Emily. "I want you to promise me that you'll eat a good dinner tonight. And breakfast tomorrow and lunch before you come to the game. Okay?"

"Okay," Emily said.

Coach looked her right in the eye. "I'm serious, Emily."

"Okay," Emily said. "I promise."

"You don't want to faint on the field, do you?"

"No," Emily told her. "I'm sorry."

"There's nothing to be sorry about," Coach said. "Just take care of yourself. I'm going to call your mother when I get home. Meantime, you tell her what happened, okay?"

Emily nodded, said thank you again, and got out of the car.

Tears sprang to her eyes. I am fat, she told herself. And now I have to eat so I don't faint. I'll stay fat, and I'll never be a good cheerleader.

BLUE HERON DRIVE 10:00 P.M.

Sally locked her bedroom door and went to her closet. It was time to prepare for the big game tomorrow, and she didn't want her mother, father, or little brother to walk in on her.

She pulled out the duffel bag she'd used for camp. She'd been planning this prank since last summer. Thank you, Liz, she thought as she opened the bag and took out the three little packets that would release a truly disgusting odor into the visiting cheerleaders' bathroom. Liz Cioffi, her bunk mate, had brought stink bombs to camp thinking it would be a fun trick to play on another cabin. In what she considered one of her more brilliant moves, Sally convinced Liz not to use them. "It's a little childish," she'd told her. "I'll hide them so you won't be tempted."

By the end of camp Liz had totally forgotten about the stink bombs, and Sally had the perfect prank to pull on the Cougar cheerleaders. Not big and splashy like vandalizing buses. But it was something. The best part was that no one knew her plan. She was doing this solo.

She stashed the stink bombs in the bottom of her cheerleading bag.

If she was really lucky the school bus prank would still happen, but without Darryl. The high school guys might be spray-painting the buses right now. Yes, it could all work out just fine.

The other cheerleaders might have forgiven the Cougar squad for what happened at the game last year. But they weren't humiliated the way she was.

It was halftime in the game, and the Cougars were ahead. The Cougar cheer squad did an extralong center cheer, so there were only a few minutes left in halftime when the Bulldogs ran out for their turn. Thirty seconds into the routine Sally's bases threw her up in a Free Heel Stretch. **"Go, Bulldogs!"** she shouted.

At that instant some members of the Cougar

band did an extraloud trumpet and drum fanfare. The bases holding Sally were so startled by the surprising interruption that they loosened their hold on her. She wobbled at the top of the pyramid in front of *hundreds* of people. From her high vantage point she saw Cougar cheerleaders laughing at her as she tried to keep her balance and shout the cheer. The fanfare played again. Then a few of the musicians broke into a swing number. A lot of Cougar fans were shouting, "Win, Cougars, Win!"

Bulldog fans tried to shout the Cougar fans down. But it only added to the noise and confusion.

Lisa, the co-captain of the Bulldogs cheer squad, must have given the signal to stop the cheer and leave the field. By then Sally's bases were off count, so the timing of her Full-Twist Dismount was off. The dismount was awkward and scary. And no one noticed that she lost her balance as soon as she hit the ground. They were already running back to the sidelines.

Sally was alone in the middle of the Cougar field. The Cougar fans were applauding because they had stopped the Bulldogs' halftime cheer, and they were laughing at the cheerleader sitting on the ground.

As she ran — alone — off the field, Sally saw that those Cougar cheerleaders were still laughing at her. By the time she joined her squad at the sidelines, the Cougar coach was talking to Coach Cortes. She apologized for what a few band members did and said that Bulldog cheerleaders should go back out and do the halftime cheer.

Coach Cortes said there wasn't enough time left and the crowd was too riled up. That the best thing would be to go on with the game. They talked some more about what had happened, and later Coach Cortes told her squad that only a few people in the band were responsible. But Sally knew better. She saw the cheerleaders laughing, and she remembered how they had tried to shout over the Bulldog sideline cheers.

It was time for revenge.

CMS GIRLS' LOCKER ROOM. SATURDAY 12:30 P.M.

It was one hour until kickoff. Mrs. Johnson was putting sparkles in Emily's hair. "Your hair is adorable that way," she told her.

Emily tried to smile. She had followed Coach's instructions, but she couldn't help feeling really fat. She'd eaten a big meal last night and had breakfast and lunch today.

"What's wrong, sweetheart?" Mrs. Johnson asked as she dabbed a few sparkles on Emily's cheek. "You look all worried."

"Mrs. Johnson, do you think my uniform fits okay?" Emily asked.

"Call me *Sally Sue*, dear," she said. "Now turn around and let me see."

Emily turned around slowly in front of Mrs. Johnson. "I'd say it fits perfectly," she said. "But that's how I like to see the uniforms — nice and snug."

Sally's mother thinks my uniform is snug, too, Emily thought. And I ate so much for dinner last night. I have to go back on a diet.

"Could you give Sally a message for me?" Sally Sue asked Emily, interrupting her thoughts.

"Sure," Emily answered.

"Tell her that I have her cheerleading shoes. She forgot them at home, so I brought them with me. I'm afraid she'll think they're still at home."

Emily went back to the hall where some of the cheerleaders were warming up. Sally wasn't there.

Melody, who had been keeping a lookout for the arrival of the Santa Rosa school buses, came out of one of the classrooms and walked over to Emily.

"They're not here yet," Melody whispered to Emily.

"I hope nothing happened to those buses," Emily said.

"I'll check again in a few minutes," Melody told her.

"Have you seen Sally?" Emily asked.

"I think I saw her going down the hall a minute ago," Melody said as she slowly lowered herself into a split.

"If she comes back, tell her that her mother has her shoes," Emily said. "But I'll try to find her."

As Emily walked away, she felt a wet lick on her calf. "Bubba," she giggled as she turned and looked down. Bubba wagged his behind and licked Emily's calf again. He seemed very proud of himself, all decked out in his CMS T-shirt and fancy dog collar.

Some of the cheerleaders called out, "Hi, Bubba." And, "Isn't he cute?"

Emily's mother was right behind him. "Can I leave him with you for a few minutes?" she asked. "Your father will be here soon."

"Sure," Emily said.

"You look great, honey," Mrs. Granger said as she handed Emily Bubba's leash. "Just perfect. The stands are already filling up. Good luck."

"Come on, Bubba," Emily told her dog. "We're going to go find Sally."

Emily and Bubba walked quickly down the length of the hall. Sally wasn't there or in any of the classrooms along the way. I hope she didn't go home to get her shoes, Emily thought. If she gets there and can't find them she'll really panic. Plus she might miss the start of the game.

"Let's check downstairs," she told Bubba.

When they got to the first-floor corridor, Bubba barked. Emily saw Sally at the other end of the corridor in front of the bathroom that was reserved for the Cougar cheer squad.

Sally almost jumped out of her skin when she heard Bubba's bark and saw him and Emily running toward her. She put her cheerleading bag over her shoulder and held it against her side.

"Hi," Emily called out. "I was looking for you."

"What's up?" asked Sally.

"It's about your bag," Emily said.

Does she know I have stink bombs in there? Sally wondered. How could she? "What about my bag?" asked Sally as she clutched it closer.

"Well, if you look in there you'll see that you forgot your shoes," Emily said. "Your mother asked me to tell you that she has them."

"I figured she had them," Sally said. "But thanks anyway."

Bubba pulled on the lead and tried to jump up on Sally.

Emily yanked him back. "Bubba likes you," she told Sally.

Oh, right, thought Sally.

Bubba tried again to jump to Sally's bag.

Sally backed away. How could she get rid of this silly seventh-grader and her ugly dog?

A huge smile spread across Emily's face. "I know why you're down here," she said. "You're welcoming the visiting cheerleaders. That is so great! Can Bubba and I stay and help?"

Sally's heart sank. There was no way she could pull off her prank. Even if Emily and the dog left now, it wouldn't work. Emily had seen her in front of the bathroom for the Cougar cheer squad. Besides, time was running out. The Santa Rosa buses would soon be here. If Emily had come just a minute later, she thought, it would have been a close call.

Suddenly the air filled with an awful smell. Panic raced through Sally's body. Had one of the stink bombs gone off in her bag? How could it without a match?

Emily smelled it, too, and flushed with embarrassment. "Sorry," she said. "Bubba farted. Bulldogs do that a lot."

Just then Melody ran up to them. "Oh, Bubba! Phew!" she exclaimed.

Sally snuck a sniff of her bag. The terrible smell wasn't coming from there. She glanced down at Bubba and thought, He's ugly *and* he farts.

The doors at the end of the corridor opened,

and a stream of girls dressed in black-and-red cheer uniforms spilled into the hall.

"The buses are clean," Melody quickly whispered in Emily's ear. "No pranks."

"Great!" Emily whispered back. Then she shouted hi to the visiting cheerleaders. "Welcome to CMS."

"Hi," a few of the Cougar cheerleaders shouted back.

"Thanks," someone else said.

A pretty girl with shiny black hair ran up to them. "You're Sally, aren't you?" the girl said to Sally.

"Yes," Sally said. She put on her biggest fake smile.

"I'm Cassie Jimenez," the girl said. "Thanks for coming down to meet us." Bubba gave a little bark and wagged his behind.

Cassie squatted down to pet him. "Bubba is so cute," she gushed. "We all feel just awful about what happened with that stuffed animal. Some graduates of SRMS and maybe one or two of the football players did it. But, well, we apologize even though we didn't have anything to do with it."

"Thanks for saying that," Sally said.

"No one thought it was the cheerleaders' fault," Melody added.

"We owe you an apology for last year, too,"

Cassie said, "for not keeping things under control during halftime. We had a nasty co-captain. It was all her idea to shout during your cheers. But it's different this year. We read what you wrote in the paper and totally agree with you. Our coach is talking to your coach right now. She greeted us at the bus. That was really nice."

"I'm so glad," Sally said through a frozen smile.

Emily couldn't believe her good luck. She'd been here to be part of the coming together of the Bulldog and Cougar cheer squads. There would be peace between the cheerleaders at the football game.

Sally looked at the grinning faces of the visiting cheerleaders. "I better get back to my squad," she said. She flashed one last fake smile, turned, and left.

She couldn't bear to smile at those girls for one more second.

CMS FOOTBALL FIELD 1:30 P.M.

Joan was the first to run out onto the field. She looked up at the stands packed with fans. On one side blue-and-white banners waved for the Bulldogs. On the other she saw flashes of red and black. Plenty of Cougar fans had come to the game, too.

104

The Bulldog fans applauded and shouted as their cheerleaders filed out and formed an arch of blue-and-white pom-poms. A few Cougars booed, but the Bulldog cheers drowned them out.

"And now, Bulldog fans, welcome YO-OUR players!" the announcer shouted over the loudspeaker.

The Bulldog fans rose to their feet and cheered as their football players ran onto the field, between the two rows of cheerleaders.

When Darryl passed Melody he smiled and winked. She smiled back. Everyone was ready for a great game.

The Bulldogs lined up on the track in front of their fans and waited for the Cougars. The Cougar cheerleaders and players ran onto the field, and the Cougar fans were on their feet.

"Please all stand for the national anthem," the announcer instructed.

Everyone in the stands stood at attention with the players and cheerleaders.

After the Pledge of Allegiance the fans sat down, and the referees and football captains tossed a coin to see which side would kick off.

The Bulldogs won the toss, and Randy kicked the ball into play.

Before the first quarter was over the Bulldogs made their first touchdown.

Joan, Mae, C.J., and Sally tumbled as the rest of the squad shook their pom-poms and shouted:

Touchdown. X
Touchdown. X
The Bulldogs scored a
touchdown. X X

Darryl kicked for the extra point, and Melody did an individual cheer for him while a base of cheerleaders threw Joan up in a Free Liberty. Sally walked up and down the sidelines with the other cheerleaders keeping the crowd pumped up, but she kept her eye on Melody Max.

Alexis sat in the stands with Jake, Adam, and some of their friends. She held her slender reporter's notebook in one hand and a pencil in the other.

"Isn't this great?" Jake asked her.

"Yeah," she said. "I like watching the cheerleaders as much as the football game."

"I meant, 'Isn't it great that the buses didn't get vandalized?'" Jake said. "I bet what you wrote helped."

Alexis turned to him and smiled. "You think so?"

"Yeah," Jake said, returning her smile.

"It also helped that your grandmother found

out which high school kids were going to do it," said Alexis.

"Uh-oh!" Adam exclaimed.

Alexis and Jake looked back to the field.

The Cougars had scored a touchdown. Alexis watched nervously as they kicked for the extra point. The score was tied.

When it was four minutes to halftime the Cougars were moving toward another touchdown. The cheerleaders walked up and down in front of the crowd, shouting:

Hold that line! X X
Hold that line! X X

The Cougars didn't advance.

At halftime the score was still tied. It was time for the Bulldog center cheer. As the girls ran out to the field the dance music for their halftime cheer came over the loudspeaker. They started with a stunt. Melody heard some boos from the Cougar side. But other fans and the Cougar cheerleaders were telling them to quiet down.

The Bulldog cheerleaders came out of the stunt and went into the tumbling section of their routine.

After the tumbling, the girls spread out for

the dance portion of their routine. They ended with pyramids and screamed, **"Fight, Bulldogs, Fight!"** The Bulldog fans were on their feet, clapping.

As she ran off the field Emily noticed that even some Cougar fans were applauding. She felt her heart pound and sweat break out on her forehead. The center cheer was a lot of work.

"Over here," Mae told Emily. "Coach said to line up and watch the Cougar cheerleaders. As a good example to the rest of the crowd."

The Cougar cheerleaders were good. Emily decided that Cassie was the best. She was tiny like Joan and a great tumbler and flyer. It must be wonderful to be so small, she thought.

During the third quarter the Cougars scored another touchdown, but they missed the extra point.

At the end of the third quarter the score was Cougars 13, Bulldogs 7.

Joan was hoarse from yelling, but that didn't stop her. **"G-O, let's go, Bulldogs. G-O, let's GO,"** she shouted.

And the Bulldogs did go. In the final thirty seconds of play Darryl scored a touchdown. The score was tied. Melody started to run out to do her individual cheer for Darryl when she felt a hand pull her back. "A captain should do this one," Sally said.

"Of course," Melody told her. "Go ahead."

Sally tumbled out to the sideline and did her cheer with a series of jumps.

The Bulldog fans went wild yelling Darryl's name.

If he made the extra point they'd win the game. Darryl kicked. Emily watched the ball fly between the goalposts.

The band played the school song.

The game was over. Bulldogs 14, Cougars 13.

The Bulldog football players ran up to the Cougar players and shook hands. Emily bent over and picked up Bubba so he could be part of the excitement, too.

"DAR-RYL. DAR-RYL," the Bulldog fans shouted.

The CMS cheerleaders jumped up and down, shouting and hugging. Sally turned to hug the cheerleader behind her. "We did it!" she shouted. The cheerleader she faced was Emily, and she was holding Bubba, who gave Sally a slobbering lick on the cheek.

"Isn't it great!" shrieked Emily.

Sally flashed Emily a forced grin before turning to wipe the slobber off her cheek with the back of her hand. She looked around for Darryl and saw him looking for her. That was her Bulldog!

BULLDOG CAFÉ
5:00 P.M.

Emily, Joan, Melody, Adam, Alexis, and Jake went back to the café after the game. They took a big table near the railing. Jake and Emily went to the kitchen for a pitcher of fruit punch and a big platter of burritos.

"I'm so hungry," Joan said as she took a burrito. "I always get hungry when I cheer."

"Me, too," said Melody as she bit into a burrito.

Emily poured juice for everyone. I won't eat a burrito, she promised herself. I'm starting my diet again right now.

"There's Darryl and Sally," Jake said.

Everyone turned and saw Darryl and Sally walking arm in arm down the street. When they came closer Emily invited them to join the party.

"We're going to a beach party and — " Sally started to say.

"Hey, burritos," Darryl said, interrupting her. "Man, those look good." He climbed over the rail onto the deck before Sally could object. There's no getting out of this now, she thought. Not when Darryl saw free food. She put two hands on the rail and swung herself over.

Jake made room for Darryl to pull up a chair between him and Melody. And Joan made space for Sally between her and Emily. Jake gave each of the newcomers a plate and napkin. Joan poured them juice.

Emily handed the plate of burritos to Sally. "No, thanks," Sally said. Emily was glad she hadn't taken one herself.

"That was one great game, Darryl," Melody said. "You were awesome."

"Thanks," he said. He leaned toward her and whispered, "You gave me some good advice. Thanks."

"I was afraid you were angry at me," she whispered back.

"Nah," he said. "Not really." He smiled and their gaze locked for an instant.

He really is cute, thought Melody. Maybe Big T is right about guys and crushes. Maybe it wouldn't be so bad to have one special guy.

When Melody turned back to face the others she thought Sally was glaring at her. But maybe it was just the way the sun was hitting her sunglasses.

"So where do you hang out when you're not being a cheerleader?" Darryl asked Melody.

"Here at Emily's sometimes," Melody said. "Sometimes people come to my place. Our apartment complex has a pool and tennis courts."

"You play tennis?" he asked.

"I love tennis," Melody told him. As she said

it she had a memory of playing with her father in Miami. They'd played doubles in a celebrity tournament for charity and made it through the semifinals. "Maxi and I have played together since she could hold a racket," her father told the sportscaster covering the event for the evening news. She really missed her weekly tennis games with her father.

"Maybe I'll come by some time and we could play," Darryl told her.

"Okay with me," Melody said.

"Joanie, you did great today," Sally said. "Sam Paetro is going to love working with you."

Sally would never say anything to me about being good, thought Emily, because I'm not good. She looked around at everyone at the table. This was one of those spontaneous after-game parties like her sister used to have. Now she was having one. It was her dream come true. Only in the dream she didn't imagine herself as a fat, not very good cheerleader. But that's what I am, she thought sadly.

Alexis glanced over at Emily and noticed that she was twisting a curl around her index finger — a sure sign that she was upset about something. What is bothering her? Alexis wondered. Usually when something was bothering Emily, she would talk to Alexis about it. She hoped that Emily would ask her and not anyone else to sleep over. That would be a perfect time to talk and be close like they used to be.

Emily looked up and saw Alexis staring at her and smiled. I miss Alexis, she thought. Alexis was right. We're not as close since we don't see each other as much. She thought about inviting Alexis for a sleepover and decided against it. When they had a sleepover they did loads of snacking. And tonight she was back on her diet.

HARBOR DRIVE 10 P.M.

Alexis walked past her mother sitting on the couch. "I'm going to bed now," Alexis said.

"You don't want to stay up and watch a movie with me?" her mother asked. She held up a video. "It's about a guy who has to keep living the same day over and over again." She sighed. "Sometimes I feel that's the way my life is. Too bad my life's not a comedy. Anyway, the movie is supposed to be funny. That's what the video guy said."

"I'm pretty tired," Alexis said as she bent over and kissed her mother good night. She was tired, but mostly she wanted to be alone to think.

Alexis went upstairs to her room. I hope Mom watches a movie and doesn't bother me, she thought as she closed the door behind her. She put on her nightgown, went to the window, and looked out at the sky. I wonder what Jake's doing, she thought. Maybe he stayed late at the Grangers' and was watching a movie with Emily and her whole family. Alexis wished again that Emily had asked her to stay over.

Emily seemed so different now that she was on the cheer squad. Alexis wondered what was wrong with her friend. Things just didn't seem right with Emily or the two of them.

Alexis turned from the window and went over to her desk. The copy of the *Bulldog Edition* lay open to her article. She loved seeing her name in print. Being a reporter was great. But not if she couldn't share it with her best friend.

DOLPHIN COURT APARTMENTS
10:30 P.M.

Melody Max stood on the terrace overlooking the pool, watching the reflections change as the water rippled in the breeze. She remembered how Sally took her turn cheering for Darryl. It's like we're sharing him, she thought. Only Sally's the one at a beach party right now. When they were all at the Bulldog Café had Sally really glared at her? Why? Melody wondered. Doesn't she like me?

If I was in Miami I could talk to Tina about Sally and Darryl, Melody thought. She hadn't talked to Emily, Joan, and Alexis about Darryl.

Now that she thought about it they didn't talk about boys much at all. But Tina did — all the time. She'd already told Tina a little bit about Darryl. But she hadn't told her about the weird vibes she'd been getting from Sally.

She sighed and went back inside.

Maybe it was all her imagination.

DELHAVEN DRIVE 10:45 P.M.

Joan's father pulled the car into the driveway. Her parents were in the front seat, and she and Adam were in the back. They were coming back from a piano concert in Fort Myers.

"That was an amazing performance," Joan's father said as he turned off the engine.

It *was* amazing, Joan thought as she got out of the car. The pianist had given an all-Chopin performance. And Chopin was her favorite composer. The music still rang through her mind.

"I loved it," Joan told her mother as they walked toward the house. "It was awesome."

"I'm sure he practiced more than a half hour a day," her father said as he unlocked the back door.

"And didn't spend all day Saturday at sporting events," her mother added.

"How do you know?" Joan said.

"Maybe he played football *and* practiced the piano," Adam said. "Some people can manage their time very well." Joan threw him a grateful smile.

Her mother turned on the kitchen light. "Someone who is serious about the piano doesn't play football," she said. "Even if he had the time for it, which he wouldn't, he has to protect his hands. A broken wrist can ruin a promising career."

"But — " Joan began.

"That's why we wouldn't let you do gymnastics, Joanie," her father said, interrupting her. "There are so many small bones in the hand and wrist. A young man I knew in college who was so gifted as a violinist — "

"Jared Capek," her mother put in.

"I know about Jared," Joan said. "You already told me about a thousand times."

"So I have," her father said. He smiled at his family. "Anyone want tea?"

"No, thanks," Joan said. She didn't say she was tired, because then they'd say she shouldn't have been at the football game. Instead she said, "Thanks for taking us to the concert. I loved it."

She said good night and went to her room.

I love cheering, and I love the piano, she thought as she closed her door. And I'll do both. I will.

THE MANOR HOTEL.
11:00 P.M.

Emily closed the door to her room. It had been a perfect day. First the game. Next the spontaneous party at the café. Then Jake stayed for dinner.

She looked out the window and saw Jake walking home alone in the moonlight. Tonight they both laughed so hard at a video that tears ran down their faces. Too bad Alexis wasn't here, Emily thought. She'd have loved that movie, too.

Emily put both hands on her stomach. It was puffed out again. She'd wanted to have only salad for dinner. But since the coach had talked to her mother she couldn't get away with it. Her mother insisted she have meat and rice, too. The only meal I can skip now, she thought, is lunch.

There was a tap on her door. "Who is it?" she called.

"Me," answered her mother's voice. "And Bubba."

"Come in," Emily answered.

Her mother came in carrying an old dress box. She put the box on the bed and sat beside it.

Bubba licked Emily's calf. "Hello to you, too," she said as she leaned over and patted his head.

117

"You looked terrific out there today," her mother said. "Was it fun?"

"It was great," Emily answered. "What's in the box?"

Her mother opened the box and held up a short blue-and-white dress.

"What's that?" Emily asked.

Her mother stood up and turned the dress around. Across the front of the top Emily read CMS. "It's my CMS uniform," her mother said.

"I've seen pictures of you in that uniform," said Emily. "I didn't know you still had it."

"How do you think I looked in those photos?" her mother asked. "The truth."

"You looked great," Emily said.

"Did I look fat?" her mother asked.

" 'Course not," answered Emily.

Her mother handed Emily the uniform. "Try it on," she said.

"It'll be too small," Emily protested.

"Try it," her mother insisted.

Emily took off her jeans and shirt. Her mother handed her the uniform, and Emily dropped it over her head. It smelled musty from the attic.

"The zipper is in the back," her mother said. "I'll do it."

"It won't close," Emily told her.

"Don't be so sure," her mother commented.

Emily held her breath as she felt the cool zipper moving upward along her spine.

"For goodness sake, breathe, Emily," her mother said as she closed the hook and eye at the top of the zipper. "It fits fine."

Emily let out her breath. Her mother was right. The uniform fit her perfectly.

Emily looked up and saw her reflection in her bureau mirror. She looked just like her mother in those photos. The same red hair. The same body.

"Now, will you stop this foolish dieting?" her mother asked. "And eat right."

Emily nodded.

After she'd given her mother back the uniform, she put on her nightgown. She was exhausted and ready to go to bed, but there was one more thing she had to do. She picked up her own cheerleading uniform from the chair, clipped the skirt to the hanger, slipped the top over the hanger, and put it in her closet.

She'd only cheered for one game. There would be a lot more pep rallies and games to cheer for before her uniform would be stored in the attic. The new Bulldog cheerleaders had a whole lot of cheerleading to do.

ABOUT THE AUTHOR

Jeanne Betancourt has written many novels for young adults, several of which have won Children's Choice awards. She also writes the popular Pony Pal series for younger readers.

Jeanne lives in New York City and Sharon, Connecticut, with her husband, two cats, and a dog. Her hobbies include drawing, painting, hiking, swimming, and tap dancing. Like the girls in CHEER USA, she was a cheerleader in middle school.

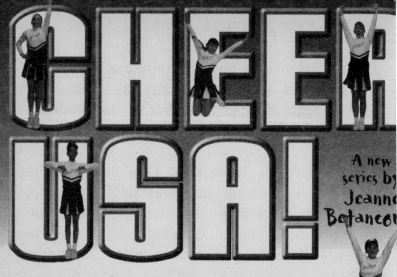

CHEER USA!

A new series by Jeanne Betancourt

They've got spirit, How 'bout you?

$4.50 each!

- ❑ BDL0-590-97806-3 **#1: Go, Girl, Go!**
- ❑ BDL0-590-97808-X **#2: Fight, Bulldogs, Fight!**
- ❑ BDL0-590-97809-8 **#3: Ready, Shoot, Score!**
- ❑ BDL0-590-97876-4 **#4: We've Got Spirit!**